THE EVE YEARS
OF
REFORMATION

NAOMY NJERI HYVÖNEN

ISBN 978-1-968970-28-4 (Paperback)
ISBN 978-1-968970-29-1 (Ebook)

Inquiries and Book Orders should be addressed to:

Leavitt Peak Press
17901 Pioneer Blvd Ste L #298, Artesia, California 90701
Phone #: 2092191548

Contents

PART 1

The Shadow of
the Empire

1920-1958

For my mother,
Whose storytelling painted vivid pictures
of her childhood in Njoro,
bringing me into her lively family of many siblings,
as though I had grown up among them.
And for my late father,
who relished my endless questions,
recounting our nation's history, after long journeys
from the remote regions of East Africa
where his work as a pastor took him -
because in me, he found a tireless listener.
Thank you, from the bottom of my heart.

Chapter 1

Muriuki

Muriuki sat outside the thatched hut. He sat on his three-legged stool that had seen many better days. Today was the beginning of another life, an unpredictable life. He could hear commotion here and there in the compound. The boys were hustling over things, trying to gather what they could carry with them to the adjoining part of the land that would now be their home.

'*Múriúki!*' Wangu called from the kitchen. It was becoming increasingly difficult for her to move around now. She knew that he did not mind being bothered with the smallest chores.

'*Níkíi Wangú?*' [what is it Wangu?] He started as he rose from his stool. He was not very young anymore, and this amounted to the problem. He had slid down a slope during their last hunting season and now he suffered a bad back so that he could not rise as fast as he wished.

'*Nengera marigú maya Múriúki wakwa.*' [hand me these bananas, my Muriuki] She began. Bananas had always been her favourite fruit and now in her last weeks of pregnancy they were all she ate. Muriuki handed her two bananas and sat across from her.
'*Ciana rí.*' [What about the children]
'*Ciana cií wíra.*' [The children are working]

'*íí ríu Múriúki í, gúgúthií atía?*' [What will happen now Muriuki?]

Muriuki did not know what to say. He looked over at Wangu and could not hold eye contact. He had lost two of his three wives due to disease, and had maintained his decision not to take another wife besides Wangu. Or perhaps he had not been man enough, as some had said.

'Every Kikuyu man needs a household of wives and many sons and daughters. One wife is not enough to hold your homestead. Don't you know that wives are the pillars of your stead, and one pillar is not sufficient?' Kinyanjui had once said.

Muriuki had answered without thinking, 'I thought we are the pillars of our stead. In which case, we are enough.'

But Kinyanjui, known for his sharp tongue, had sat up and with a pointed finger had stated, 'we are the foundation, on which the pillars are built.'

Muriuki smiled vaguely as he watched his pregnant wife swallow the last of her banana. Wangu meant everything to him. But now he had lost everything he had built up for her and for the children.

'*Tiga kúmaka.*' [Do not worry] He said to Wangu. But he too was worried. Like so many Kenyans he had lost his land to a European settler. What was worse was the loss of his brothers who had joined the British Army in the First World War and never returned home. Their land had perished with them, and now, incapable of looking after his brothers' families, Muriuki felt shame. There was no consolation for this.

'*Míaka íno yothe tútúríte haha í, no ríu tu Múthúngú ona atútunye múgúnda?*' [all these years we have dwelt here, why is it that now the white man takes away our land?]

But Muriuki could not answer this either. He had struggled, as many had done before him, but they had lost. No amount of European education or sturdy houses could compensate for the dispossession of land.

The dawn of the twentieth century had ushered in a tide of European settlers and missionaries into Kenya. Yet, for most

Kenyans, the distinction between the two was nebulous at best. In the minds of many, the identities of settler and missionary coalesced into one - *mzungu*, the white man, whose presence embodied power and territorial conquest. It became a profound contradiction, bewildering yet resignedly accepted. The Europeans' way of life stood in stark contrast to the customs of the African communities. This dissonance was impossible to ignore.

Many Kenyans were converting to Christianity, though there remained a large proportion that maintained traditional beliefs and practices. Muriuki was one of the converts. It happened that shortly after moving into the servants' quarters, Wangu went into labour. Mrs. Donovan called for a midwife just before dawn, and a healthy Justus Muriuki was born. Perhaps it was this simple act of kindness, this human connection in a time of need, that slowly opened Muriuki's heart to the Christian faith.

Across the country, many Kenyans that had been dispossessed of their land and livelihoods were desperately searching for work and shelter. Among them were Muriuki's own extended family - his late brothers' wives and their children - who now faced an uncertain future. Groups of people, especially the young, often travelled great distances on foot in the hope of finding food and employment. Tragically, many succumbed to disease and malnutrition along the way. Despite his own hardships, Muriuki offered support to some of these wanderers in search of survival.

Chapter 2

Justus Muriuki

What Justus lacked in his life was growing up in his and his brothers' inheritance, as was customary for the Kikuyu people. Land was an essential part of Kikuyu culture and losing it was shameful and abhorrent.

'*Múgúnda ní ta nguo*' [Land is like the clothing you wear] His father used to say. You lose it and you are a naked man. For many years in his youth, Justus had wondered why his father had not fought harder to retrieve his land. He was witness to many deprived Kenyans that roamed the countryside searching for survival and who ended up at their home where they were nurtured and fed for days before they resumed their search. His older brothers had married and left the servants' quarters long before he was old enough to run. His father told him, '*Nímeyoneire wíikaro Kínangopu*' [they found dwelling in Kinangop]. It was many years before he went to visit them in Kinangop - only to discover to his horror that they too lived in a settler's land, in servants' quarters like his parents.

His life, however, was more promising than his brothers'. His father saw to it that he got an education, something neither he nor his older sons had received. Although he did not understand it himself, Muriuki thought if it was good for the settler, it would be good for his youngest son. So he sent Justus to school at an early age. Mr. Donovan was quick to see potential in the boy, and after taking him under his wing, he sent him off to London in 1938 to study law.

The Second World War broke out a year later, and was felt everywhere in the British colonies. One of Muriuki's sons, Kamau, and three grandsons were recruited in the King's African Rifles, which had gradually grown in numbers, protecting the entire Eastern African region that belonged to Britain. Muriuki's grandsons had been recruited first. They were strong young men and the army desperately needed to increase in numbers. Kamau had forced his way into the Rifles, to protect his nephews.

'What right do they have to take our young men to war?' He'd argued with his brothers. Kamau had only daughters, and the anguish of losing his nephews - young men forced to fight in a war none of them understood - ignited a rage that consumed him. Powerless to stand by, he enlisted.

Justus had known nothing of his nephews and brother fighting against the Italian troops, until mid 1940, through a letter from one of his nieces, Martha, the only one that could read and write besides himself in their family. In Britain, intelligence agencies made haste to recruit leading experts in their respective fields, to make use of their knowledge for war efforts, and therefore there had been a huge shortage of lecturers. With shortened lessons, Justus had accepted work to tutor the children of a wealthy Greek family in West London. When many young men began to leave universities to serve in the war, Justus begun to consider returning home. But bombings in London forced an evacuation of remaining students and many workers at the universities. They were relocated to Cambridge. He wrote a letter to Martha:

'We were evacuated to Cambridge last week, about 100 km from London. A building next to our college came down after a bombing in the night. A few people died, dozens injured, but the fear is the worst. Like thick smoke. You can smell it and feel it. I am trying to get my way back home. It is impossible to remain here. Most British men have gone to service. A few of us are stranded here, feeling useless. How is everyone? Do you get news of the ongoing war?'

To which many weeks later Martha had replied and informed him that his brother Kamau and his oldest nephews were then fighting against the Italian troops. She also added that his father was visiting Kinangop and when he heard that she was replying to his letter, had warned him to not return to 'this uncontrolled insanity and drought.'

It was impossible for him to afford his ticket to Kenya anyway, and he remained in Cambridge, eventually enrolling in the city's fire brigade because of the growing need for firefighters. He was walking home one night with Henry, whose hand was on his arm because he could barely see in the dark.

'Do you ever think what would become of us if Germany invaded England?' Justus asked. The fear of German invasion was all over, especially in London. It seemed that every activity by His Majesty's government was geared toward preventing an invasion.

Henry shrugged. 'I refuse to entertain such thoughts.'

He was built for gentler times, unable to stand firm when it mattered. Lucky for him, his bad eyesight had rendered him unfit for any useful service, sparing him the brutal demands of the battlefield. He was assigned to menial tasks such as helping load and unload things at the fire station. They were amongst the dwindling number of male students left, in a sea of female students.

'Well,' Justus informed, 'I do.'

'What do you mean?'

'I mean I think about where I'd hide.' Justus sheepishly grinned nodding at the group of female students walking out of a building, as they approached their students' quarters.

'You what?' Grimaced Henry.

'C'mon Henry. Tell me you wouldn't want to hide where they'd hide.'

Henry was silent. He squinted as hard as he could to watch the girls walk away. Then he chuckled, 'I don't suppose I'd mind!'

They were sitting in Hersch Lauterpacht's crowded lecture one afternoon, when Henry leaned over and whispered, 'a letter addressed to you arrived earlier. From Kenya.' Justus could feel the contents of the letter even before he read it. He looked around the auditorium, now full of '*strangers without gowns*'. Academic refugees. Bright minds from everywhere - Soviet Union, China, Spain, Germany and other countries. Jewish intellectuals, anti-Franco republicans, emigres fleeing Bolshevik Revolution, anti-fascists fleeing Mussolini's regime and elite Chinese students of law. They were forced together in a lecture room in Cambridge, far from their own colleges because of the war. He thought of the war going on in Kenya. The Italian army, made up of more than 200 000 soldiers invading British East Africa, and disarming an army of no comparable size.

His brother and nephews had perished at the Lake Rodolfo onslaught, said Martha, an ambush from the Italian army and the Daasanach tribe who lived in the region.

That evening as he sat on the bed with the letter in his hand, thinking of his brother and nephews, there came a loud knock on the door. Henry bolted upright from where he lay on the bed, shot Justus a glance then jumped up at the second knock.

'Mr. Muriuki?'

Henry moved aside.

'Sir?' Justus answered.

Two soldiers stood at the doorway. One of them handed him a letter. As Justus pulled out the contents, the soldier who handed him the letter said, 'You have been conscripted Mr. Muriuki, and are expected to report to duty tomorrow. A bus will be waiting in the morning at 8am, at the address indicated. Welcome to service.'

Justus took the outstretched hand. 'Sir?'

'Yes?'

'I'm not a British citizen. Sir. I'm a student from Kenya.' He started, bewildered, and searching for Henry to intervene.

'It is well understood that you're from a British colony. You're one of us. You'll be fighting against German imperialism in your service, Mr. Muriuki. Good evening gentlemen.'

With the door shut, Justus slumped on his bed, 'Fighting against German imperialism - and the freedom of Britain. Without a gun.'

Henry took the letter. Read through. 'Blimey, look where they're sending you, you lucky sod!' But Justus was thinking of his bad luck.

'Two letters in one day, delivering bad news!'

'Think of it this way. There'll be hundreds upon hundreds of women in Wales, the marrying kind, should you want to settle down.' and then, as though confiding a dark secret, 'Men in times of war are in high demand.'

But Justus did not roar with laughter as he usually would.

'You're wrong Henry. The mines in Wales are where most of the men left in Britain will be found. Everywhere else, they've been enlisted to fight the real war. With guns. Besides,' he swung his feet off the bed, 'I am not ready to settle down.'

In 1942 the British government took over the mining industry and this caused an uproar in the boarding house where Justus lived. Increased output demands to support the British war effort meant longer hours with less regard for worker rights. But that was the least of the causes for unrest. Many of the workers, including Justus, were being moved to the Forest of Dean where shortage of labour was acute. Gary, the stranded black American who'd arrived a few months earlier from France, and who was there as a regular worker, was pounding on the wall.

'No way I ain't!' he bellowed. 'I'm going back to war, that's where I'm going!'

No one quite knew his story, how he'd been estranged from his men and ended up in Wales. But there were all kinds of speculations. Justus looked at Matthew, who lay on the bed across from him.

'Where are they sending you, man?'

'Kent. You?'

'The Forest.'

They sat for dinner before dusk. Jack shouted from the kitchen, adding as usual, 'If you nah reach 'ere quick, somebody go eat up your broth!' which was often the case for the unfortunate ones. Justus had been in the kitchen, helping. It was easy to talk to Jack, and since he had a missing hand and appreciated Justus' help in the kitchen, they'd become like brothers. Jack's father had served a government official for many years in Jamaica, later relocating his family to England, by special request from the official, after the first World War. He had died shortly before the Second World War began.

'Him lucky so.' Jack sighed one Saturday evening as they sat at the corner of the dining room after dinner.

'What do you mean?' Justus asked.

'Lemme tell yuh.' Jack leaned back, looking deeply at Justus. Sometimes he reminded Justus of Mr. Donovan. Even when he did not make much sense, Jack spoke with certainty and confidence. Justus watched him, his missing hand demanding attention.

'Respect follow me father, from Jamaica come right 'ere to England. Among we own, yuh understand?' He went on, "im did want me fi take 'im work, y'see.'

Jack had been part of the militiamen, a unit that was distinguished from the regular British army and which later was absorbed into the army when the war broke out.

'See how me come drop,' he said with dismay. He'd lost his arm in 1940 in Austria during combat. 'Tell me now, wha' a man widout 'im right 'and?' He asked, his drunk eyes wide open. Despite his missing hand, Jack was the strongest man Justus knew. Although he worked as a cook and cleaned after them, he was a guardian of sorts, often stepping between fights or finishing off fights with one hand.

As he watched him, Justus wondered for a moment if there was a definition for a man without his right hand. He wondered what his father would call such a man. Then he remembered his brother, dying in the war with his nephews. He wondered who had died first. Had his nephews? If so, he imagined his brother Kamau standing there, large as a wall, commanding the Italian army to shoot him dead. Not daring to return home without his nephews. He stood up, feeling tears of anger burning in his eyes.

'Men are many things, my friend,' he stated. 'A man without his right hand is as good a man as any.'

'Wha' 'bout you, Jus?' Jack asked. 'You must waan go fight dat war back home, di one weh tek yuh brother an' yuh nephews, eh man.'

'Yea,' Justus sat back down, 'I'd do anything to finish off that war.'

But he didn't. Justus worked in the mines until the end of 1944 when he got work in a munitions factory. Many young men had by then left to join the army, and women worked in heavy jobs throughout the country. The superintendent who spotted him on a Sunday afternoon and recommended him had said, 'you'll be more useful in the factory. Too many explosions and wrong handling of chemicals calls for intelligent men.' There had been many deaths by accidents among the women that worked in factories.

While in the factory he was reunited with Henry, who ran a unit in one of the munitions factories in Wales.

'Where are you staying?'

'At a lodging.'

'You move in with us, is what you'll do, old Henry!'

And so Henry had moved in at the boarding house along river street.

Chapter 3

Rumors of War

Justus graduated from the university not long after the war was over, and returned to Kenya to work with Jade & Warsaw company in Mombasa. There were employment opportunities because many young British men who had left for war never returned. Justus couldn't imagine his luck in landing his dream job, thanks to the connections he had acquired while working in Wales.

He was walking out for lunch one afternoon with Jon, the clerk. It was his second month at Jade & Warsaw. He had rented a small apartment in a safe location, not far from Fort Jesus. He still marvelled that he was back in Kenya working as a solicitor.

'The world is your oyster,' Jon the Doctor, as everyone called him, was saying.

'The ladder is right before us, Doc.' Justus laughed. They were having *nyama choma,* at the open-air-grill under a baobab tree.

'Spoken well!' Jon exclaimed. His father, a white colonial, had been stripped of inheritance for marrying his Kenyan mother, a rare and scandalous union in the 1920s. It was an unusual story: a young white man lodging at his African in-laws, defying the rigid social order. He had humiliated his family to the extent that they moved back to England. Not long after, Jon's father vanished under mysterious circumstances leaving him, his two siblings and their mother bereft and socially adrift.

'About that ladder,' Jon lowered his voice, 'my men and I have been training, you know, in case there's a war.' Justus knew what was coming. This was not the first he'd heard about groups of men training in case of a war for independence. There were groups of men everywhere, throughout the country, training.

"We'd need ammunition, Jus,' Jon said, looking suspiciously at the other customers, who sat on stones and leaned on trees having their lunch.

'You don't know what you're talking about Doc.' He too looked around, wary of prying ears. 'I just started proper work.' Justus hissed. He owed Jon for his nice apartment. Without connections in a large city like Mombasa, one easily ended up in unsafe locations, prone to theft.

'I know. But we need you. You know ways we can get better prepared, in case of a war.'

'Listen, my friend.' They were walking back to the office. 'I have had to be separated from my family for more years than I wanted, and while I was gone I lost my brother and three nephews.'

'I hear you, my brother,'

'What I'm saying is, I want no involvement in anything considered crime,' he looked behind them, and then placed a hand on Jon's shoulder, stopping him. 'I cannot be involved.'

'Continue.'

'I know a man. He might help me to help you.'

The bar on Kilindi Road was a popular place among Kenyans, hidden beneath the hazy veil of cigarette smoke. It was here that Justus found himself immersed in a group that highly anticipated Kenya's independence. As he sat on a wooden chair, he gazed out of the window at the magnificent imperial colonial architecture lining the road. The view sharply contrasted with the battered streets of wartime London or the quiet, rain-soaked towns of Wales. Here, the buildings stood pristine, untouched by the scars of war, yet to him they seemed curiously hollow, distant from the grit and struggle he had known elsewhere.

The contrast was striking. Justus marvelled at the hints of traditional clothing worn by the residents in Mombasa. It had been days before he heard a man speak Kikuyu in the streets when he first moved here.

He sat at the table with Jon and three other men. Though bound by colonial borders, their network stretched far beyond the Kenyan coast. Indian-Kenyan traders, dockworkers, and quiet revolutionaries had opened the corridors of trust, binding Jon's group to a wider resistance. Through these alliances, they found comrades in Zanzibar, traders in Bombay, and dockworkers in Durban - men bound by a common cause although separated by seas. News of India's looming independence travelled swiftly across the Indian Ocean, stoking fires in the hearts of those who longed to see Africa unshackled from the yoke of the Empire. Their struggle was not local. It was part of a rising tide.

'The plan is to arrive before dawn at the harbour,' Jon was saying. 'James here works with the cargo. He's got the manifest, and more importantly, he knows which men are given to a quiet shilling.'

James, a lean man with sharp eyes, nodded. 'There's a ferry scheduled to dock from Aden, carrying general goods - textiles, sugar, spare parts. But tucked among the crates is a consignment of surplus ammunition, supposedly destined for settler security forces up in Nairobi. The paperwork's been fudged enough that no one will ask questions if the crates don't make it that far.'

'The dock shifts change at four-thirty in the morning. The new crew will be slower to notice movement, and the ones coming off shift will be too eager to leave.' Jon leaned in.

James continued, 'I've arranged for the shipment to be stacked near the offload point, close to the service road. At precisely four-fifty, a transport lorry - one of ours, disguised under the name of a known cargo company - will pull in for 'routine' collection. We'll have papers prepared to cover it.'

Justus, who had remained silent, raised a hand. 'What if the port authorities stop you?'

'That's where you come in, you see, because you will be there. If we get stopped, we show them the papers. If they press, you'll be there officially to represent the cargo company. You'll know the right language, the legal loopholes, the pressure points. If necessary, you will threaten them with customs violations - they don't know enough to challenge you on the spot.'

'We won't need long,' James added. 'Seven minutes to load, max. I've timed it. The lorry will head out through the western gate, where the guards will already have been 'taken care of' for that morning. From there, we split the load across several safe houses.'

Jon's voice hardened. 'Speed, silence, and no unnecessary questions. If anything goes wrong, we abandon the crates and walk away. No heroics. The mission is the cause, not the cargo.'

Justus tapped his fingers against the table, the gravity of his role settling in. 'You realise, if I misstep, you won't just lose the cargo. You'll lose men to prison.'

Jon met his gaze steadily. 'We trust you. Besides, this isn't just about a few crates of bullets. This is the beginning. For independence and for our country.'

Justus nodded, his heart pounding with a mixture of thoughts. It had been four months since that initial conversation with Jon. As a lawyer, he had the resources that made him an invaluable asset to Jon and his men. He ensured their activities remained hidden from the watchful eyes of the colonial authorities. But the magnitude of it all unnerved him.

Over the next few weeks, Justus assisted the group, using his cover to procure and move ammunition discreetly. The risks were high, but the cause they were preparing to fight for fueled his determination. The men he helped were patriots, driven by a desire for freedom from colonialism. For Jon, the drive was something even savage. The anger at losing his father, the outcast of a system that had sowed divides.

Chapter 4

Threads

The initial heist at the harbour had gone precisely as Jon had calculated. The timing - arriving just before dawn - had afforded them the shroud of half-light. James, with his knowledge of the dockyard, had guided them through the maze of stacked cargo and half-watching guards. A few other trusted men - Simon, a lorry driver with years behind the wheel and Peter, a stevedore with the muscle and wit to move unnoticed - had each played their part with quiet efficiency. Then there was Salim, whose role would be very useful.

When their father vanished, leaving Jon just old enough to remember and Salim still swaddled in his mother's arms, the village could not decide what to make of the white child with sea-green eyes. Among the Waswahili people, superstitions swirled like coastal winds. Some claimed the baby was a bad omen, a spirit misplaced among them, his white skin a sign that misfortune would follow. Others believed the misfortune had already struck, that the father's disappearance had appeased the spirits and spared the family greater sorrow.

Salim grew with the face of the coloniser but the tongue of the coast, never fully claimed by either. He often drew quiet suspicion. Among his own people, his skin and the colour of his eyes remained a question that no one dared to answer aloud. But to the resistance Salim was a blessing hidden in plain sight. His appearance would be a weapon, a figure the Empire would scarcely question.

At first, their movement of the ammunition was executed with clinical precision. The cargo was divided into smaller consignments and discreetly transported to safe houses across the city - in the backrooms of Indian-owned spice shops in Old Town, beneath the wooden counters of aging tailors, and buried behind walls of grain in the storerooms of local business people desperate for independence. These routes were known as threads, paths that were carefully planned so that even if tugged too hard, they couldn't unravel the entire mission.

But threads break.

An officer was seen prowling the harbour, asking questions. A few days later, James failed to appear at their scheduled location.

Jon's face darkened as he absorbed the news. 'Find him,' he ordered. 'If he's been caught, we're undone.'

Justus, who had once thought his role would distance him from the dirt of it all, found himself slipping to the heart of the mission. His carefully written cargo manifests were being inspected with unsettling frequency. The dockmaster, once content to wave him through with a handshake, now frowned at his documents. Small questions arose. One afternoon as he crossed Treasury Street, Lieutenant Collins, a British officer with a face like carved bone, drew alongside him.

'Busy man these days, Justus,' the officer said, with the faintest curl of amusement at the corner of his mouth.

'Honest work keeps a man out of trouble, sir,' Justus replied, his pulse thundering beneath his starched collar.

Collins paused, his pale eyes searching. 'Trouble has a way of finding busy men.'

With that, he drove off in his Land Rover.

The weight of the noose tightened. Jon called an early night council. They gathered at the small house by the railway yard, a low fire guttering in the corner. Simon sat on an upturned crate, his hands tense over his knees. Peter leaned against the doorframe, his brow furrowed.

Simon was saying quietly. 'I spoke with a man from the ferry yard. James was seen leaving with two officers three days ago.'

Jon's jaw locked. 'Dead or turned?'

Simon shook his head. 'No one knows.'

'Either way,' Jon said, 'we cannot linger. Tonight we move the final shipment inland. This is the last run.'

'And if we're stopped?' Justus drew a slow breath.

Jon's eyes burned. 'Then we will die with our eyes open.'

They dispersed for their mission. The night air was full of salt and diesel as the final consignment was loaded onto the lorry. Simon secured the crates beneath a tattered canvas. 'This one's heavier than the rest,' he muttered.

Jon gave a curt nod. 'The rifles. The rest are bullets and parts. No mistakes tonight, Simon.'

Two weeks prior Simon had misread the dockmaster's rota, nearly loading the crates onto a British naval steamer bound for Zanzibar. Had Jon not double-checked the manifests that night, their entire cache would have vanished into the sea - along with their freedoms. A single misstep now would doom them all.

Peter stood watch at the edge of the yard. Justus glanced at his watch. Midnight. They were late.

'Where's the escort truck?' Justus asked, scanning the empty street. The truck was their cover - a battered Bedford lorry driven by men from the outer ring of their network. Without the cover, the operation became perilously exposed, and worse still, it signalled the possibility of betrayal. The larger group that had pledged allegiance to their cause - dockworkers, railway porters, and job seekers from the streets - had all been drawn into the fold over months. Each man knew the cost. The failure of the escort truck to appear wasn't just a logistical snag. It was a gaping hole in their defenses. It meant that somewhere, perhaps within the very bones of their brotherhood, someone had betrayed them.

'Should've been here by now,' Simon replied, his hands tightening into fists.

Jon's eyes narrowed. 'We go without it. Sitting here waiting makes us vulnerable.'

'Doc, the plan -' Justus began.

'The plan's changed,' Jon cut in sharply. 'Get in.'

Simon climbed into the driver's seat as Justus and Jon jumped into the back, crouching among the crates. Peter slid into the passenger seat, cradling a small pistol in his lap.

The lorry roared to life and lumbered through the narrow streets of Mombasa, its tyres rattling over uneven cobblestones. They took backroads, avoiding the colonial patrol routes they had memorised over months of careful observation.

Minutes passed in silence.

Jon broke in. 'You ready Jus, if we're stopped?'

'I was born ready,' Justus shot back, his mouth dry.

Jon gave a grim chuckle. 'Good. Because tonight, you might have to buy us all our lives.'

Peter suddenly snapped his head around. 'Doctor. The tail.'

A pair of dim headlights appeared two turns back, steady, unblinking.

'Lose them,' Jon ordered.

Simon pushed the lorry harder, cutting a sharp left onto a dirt path that ran alongside the railway tracks. The pursuers followed.

'They know.' Peter growled under his breath.

'They don't know what we're carrying,' Jon said sharply. 'Only that we're running. Jus - if we're caught, this cargo is textiles. Show them the papers. Stall them.'

The headlights closed the distance.

Ahead, the tracks forked, one path leading toward the inland depot, the other toward a dead siding. Simon veered right.

'Not the siding!' Jon barked.

'We'll never outrun them on the open road,' Simon snapped. 'I've got an idea.'

The lorry shuddered as it bounced over the gravel, careening toward the siding where a line of derelict freight cars sat abandoned.

Peter flung open his door as they slowed. 'Out. Now.'

They jumped down, dragging a heavy crate with them, hearts pounding. The pursuing vehicle screeched to a halt behind them. Footsteps. Voices barking commands.

Justus cracked the crate's false top, revealing bolts of cheap cloth stacked over the weapons.

'Papers,' he whispered to himself, fumbling them out of his jacket as two officers appeared with torches.

'Halt! Step away from the cargo!'

Jon and Peter raised their hands, faces blank.

Justus stepped forward, smoothing his voice. 'Gentlemen, this shipment is for Mr. Chatur's textile shop in Old Town. Here -' he handed them the forged documents, his palm barely trembling, 'officially cleared by the customs office. Look for yourselves.'

The officers scanned the papers, their torches lingering on the bolts of cloth. One officer pried further.

'Why the detour?'

'Broken axle on the main road,' Simon lied from the cab. 'Trying to make up for lost time, sir.'

A long silence.

Finally, the officer folded the papers and handed them back. 'You're lucky we're chasing after more dangerous men tonight.'

The torches swung away, and the officers returned to their vehicle, disappearing into the night.

Justus exhaled. 'I thought that was it.'

Jon's jaw clenched. 'It almost was. We're not safe yet. We need to move this now before they come back.'

They rolled the crate onto an abandoned flatbed and pushed it down the siding toward a small storage shack that they had prepared as a fallback many weeks before.

Justus asked, 'Do you think James talked?'

Jon paused, then answered without looking at him. 'He didn't need to. The Empire has many eyes. Ours just need to be sharper.'

The night swallowed them once more as they pushed forward, ending up in Jon and Simon's room at the lodging. Jon paced the length of the narrow room, his boots creaking on the planks. 'The constables weren't chasing us by accident. They knew the route.'

A knock shattered the quiet. Three quick taps. Then two. The signal.

Peter's hand flew to his pistol as Jon crossed the room and cracked the door.

A boy, no older than ten, slipped inside, panting. He bore the red kerchief of the dock runners, the boys who carried messages between warehouses, ferries, and the streets where no colonial officer dared linger after dark.

'They're watching Jame's mother's house,' the boy whispered to Jon. 'British men. Not local police. Suits, not khaki. Men with cameras.'

The boy swallowed hard. 'And they're talking to the workers at the ferry.'

The blood drained from Justus's face. Jon pressed a few coins into the boy's hand. 'Go home. Don't speak of this.'

As the door shut, Jon's jaw tightened. 'Special Branch,' he said. 'They sent men from Nairobi.'

'They think James is part of something bigger,' Peter started. Then, 'He couldn't have talked. They know nothing!'

Jon's eyes blazed. 'Let's become *something bigger*.'

Simon frowned. 'What's that supposed to mean?'

'It means we make it real.'

Justus's heart thudded in his chest. 'Doc, if we escalate this could end our lives.'

'They're hunting us anyway, Jus! The minute they put a white officer at Jame's mother's house, the game changed.'

'The game was always theirs.'

Jon slammed his fist against the table. 'Not anymore.'

There was a beat of silence, heavy and final.

Simon broke it. 'The plan?'

Jon's eyes flicked to Justus. 'The police know we're armed, but they think we're sloppy. Tomorrow night we prove otherwise.'

'We hit the armoured convoy,' Peter said, catching the thread.

'The one moving supplies to the British officers' quarters at Fort Jesus,' Jon confirmed. 'They'll never see us coming.'

'That's madness. You're talking about an assault!' Justus paled.

Jon's voice dropped to steel. 'I'm talking about a message.'

'And James? What about him?' Peter smirked.

'If he's alive, we'll save him. If he's not, then we'll burn the men who made him talk.' He turned to Justus. 'We'll need clean papers, diversion routes, a story so tight the colonial courts will choke on it.'

Justus swallowed. 'That's asking for a miracle.'

Jon's hand clapped his shoulder. 'Good thing you're a lawyer.'

A slow smile pulled at Peter's lips. 'We're soldiers afterall.'

'We've always been soldiers,' Jon said quietly. 'Only now - they'll know our names.'

The chase had begun. The morning the convoy rolled out, Jade & Warsaw, the British firm where Justus worked, collapsed into bankruptcy. The streets outside seemed suddenly more foreign than ever.

Without a career and his hands deeper in resistance than he had ever intended, Justus took to a pen and paper, and wrote to his old friend Henry. Henry had once told him *if you ever need a door opened, find me.*

The letter was hurried and short.

There are circumstances unfolding here that may render me in need of your favour. I write not for sympathy, but for an opportunity to begin again. From wherever the call comes, I am ready to answer.

The reply was to come five weeks later.

There's a vacancy at Clifton & Radcliffe, in Nairobi. I have given my recommendation. They are expecting you.

That night, as the rain lashed the tin roofs and the storm thickened the streets, Jon's men launched their strike.

They set the fire at the storage yard, its flames licking the sky as the sirens wailed in confusion. A convoy slowed at the curve, just as Peter predicted. The fake roadblock was in place, and Justus, drenched, stepped forward waving down the first driver, slightly beginning to shake - such authority was not his to wield. There, standing beneath the beam of a lantern, was Salim, Jon's brother, his pale skin nearly glowing under the light of the lantern, a British officer's uniform hanging neatly from his frame. A cigar smouldered between his fingers, his cap pulled low to shadow the stubborn curl of his hair. He did not speak, for his tongue would betray him, the accent of Mombasa in every vowel.

Midway to the driver Justus turned, as though needing to ask something from his superior, sprinted to him, feigning deference. Salim gave a curt nod, the sort a colonial officer gave when bothered by the minor business of a native. Justus returned briskly to the waiting convoy.

'Urgent customs inspection, sir. Orders from the port authority. We'll need to verify your cargo before you proceed.'

The driver narrowed his eyes. 'At this hour?'

Justus smiled coolly, presenting the papers. 'The Empire doesn't sleep, sir.'

As the driver scanned the documents, Peter and Simon were already moving, their men slipping through the back, lifting crates from the rear of the convoy, replacing them with marked decoys.

Seconds stretched into lifetimes.

From behind a cover Jon gave the sign: *'Time's up. Pull away.'*

Justus snapped the papers back. 'Everything's in order. I suggest you proceed quickly - the roads won't stay safe in this weather.'

The British driver waved his convoy forward.

The crates of British ammunition now belonged to the resistance. By the time the authorities discovered it, the weapons were already transported inland.

Chapter 5

India's Independence

News of India's impending independence reached Kenya. It was more than international news; it signalled a critical shift in the colonial order. For those involved in Kenya's growing resistance, the event was symbolic and practical. India's success proved that the British Empire was not invincible.

The resistance group around the country quickly recognised the strategic advantage. The Indian-Kenyan community, many of whom worked at the port and on the railway lines, became increasingly valuable to the movement. Though most Indian-Kenyans did not directly participate in armed resistance, their contributions were essential. They provided logistical support, managed supply routes, and passed sensitive information through commercial and personal networks. Some were involved in financial assistance in the most discreet and effective ways.

Zanzibar's traders facilitated the movement of restricted goods. Dockworkers in Durban overlooked key shipments. Port employees in Bombay ensured safe passage for correspondence and supplies. These connections were possible because of the cultural and familial ties within the Indian diaspora and their shared opposition to colonial rule.

Justus' expertise in manipulating legal systems and producing credible forged documents reached resistance figures beyond Mombasa. Members of the Kenya African Union (KAU) in Nairobi and Kisumu began to hear of him. His skill was in subverting the colonial system from within.

Justus maintained regular correspondence with Margaret, the daughter of family friends. Margaret's perspectives on colonial rule were thoughtful, observant, and sometimes challenging. For months, he carried Margaret's letters tucked inside his pockets. With the resistance's web tightening across the country, and his name circulating in places he could no longer control, he was eager to start work in Clifton & Radcliff.

He walked the harbour one last time, speaking with the people who had quietly passed names, routes, and sealed envelopes into his hands. Men who had taught him the art of movement, how to leave no trace and ask no questions.

On August 15, 1947, India got her independence. As the Union Jack was lowered and the Indian tricolour ascended, Kenyans of Indian descent in Mombasa and Nairobi poured into the streets in spontaneous celebration joined by many native Kenyans. In the back room of Sharma's café near Mombasa's port, Jon and his circle shared the historic moment. India's first Prime Minister, Jawaharlal Nehru, had firmly rejected Lord Mountbatten's proposal to include the Union Jack in the corner of the Indian flag, a decisive break from colonial symbolism that resonated deeply with all those resisting British rule. The men in Sharma's backroom gathered around a worn wooden table, intently listening to the ongoing news over radio. Sharma's hand trembled slightly as he lifted his glass. 'Today, brothers, India stands free.'

'If they can break the chains, so can we.' Peter said as they all lifted their glasses. No one spoke of timelines or strategies then. The fall of one domino had begun.

Back at the safe house, Jon was unusually quiet. They sat on the balcony overlooking the salt breeze, sharing a flask that had been passed between them the last few years.

'You could stay,' he was saying to Justus.

'You know I can't. Nairobi needs a man like me on the inside now. You said it yourself.'

Jon's jaw tightened. 'I said we need people everywhere. I didn't say I want you there.'

The British were building thicker walls around their administration and Nairobi was no safe place. The colonial courts in the city did not bend as easily as they did in the coastal districts and other smaller towns where the resistance was spread out.

'You'll need to talk less,' Jon added. 'Men are paid to listen there. You'll be surprised who's on payroll.'

Justus gave a small laugh. 'I've been practising silence, haven't I?'

Jon's hand tightened on the flask. 'Not enough.'

Hours before he left, Salim found him packing. The younger man leaned against the open window of Justus' small living room, arms crossed, a cigarette burning low between the fingers of his right hand.

'We will see you again?' Salim asked.

'Of course.'

'I will hold you to your word.' Salim said.

There was a beat of silence between them.

'I'll keep the doors open here,' Salim continued. 'I'll play the part. Cigar in hand, polished boots, white enough for the checkpoints. But you -' His voice trailed off. 'You always had the heavier load.'

Justus's throat tightened briefly. 'You're the one carrying two skins, Salim. That's no light thing.'

Salim shrugged, flicking ash outside the window. 'I've made peace with being neither.'

He turned to go but stopped. 'Be sharp in Nairobi. They don't play fair there.'

'I know.'

'And Margaret.' Salim arched an eyebrow, his tone light but his eyes serious. 'She's writing to you for a reason, Jus. If she wants you to get out of this, do it. Don't be a fool.'

Chapter 6

The Unions

Justus felt apprehension and excitement as he stepped off the train at Nairobi's bustling station. They had expected him. Henry had ensured that. But they were not receiving him as an equal.

His desk was tucked near a drafty window that overlooked the yard where the delivery boys smoked and the secretaries had their lunch. His first file was a minor civil dispute, handed to him with polite indifference, and accompanied by a quiet instruction: *Observe. Learn.*

The British lawyers called him *Mister Muriuki,* careful to follow the letter of the profession, but the invitation was not forthcoming to their lunch table. Despite their own exclusion, the Indian clerks offered quiet nods - they understood that a lesser rung on the colonial ladder was still a rung.

Within days of his arrival a name began circling quietly around the corridors he moved through: *Harry Thuku.* The man who had once shaken the colonial foundations with mass protests in 1922. He was one of Kenya's earliest African nationalists, and had led a mass protest in Nairobi against the colonial administration's oppressive policies, particularly forced labor, high taxes, and the *Kipande system.* His arrest had sparked a massive demonstration by African supporters, which was violently suppressed by colonial police and armed settlers on March 16, 1922, leading to the deaths of at least 25 people.

After his arrest in 1922 and the massacre of his supporters, Thuku was exiled to Somalia for several years until 1931. His followers, especially those in the early trade union movements and political organizations, continued to challenge the colonial administration's policies, and were viewed by the British as subversive and dangerous.

More pressing, however, was the emerging pull of the Kenya African Union (KAU) which was gathering under men like Jomo Kenyatta, Bildad Kaggia, and Fred Kubai. It didn't take long before Justus was quietly approached.

'You're from Mombasa,' A man approached him at a cafe near River Road.

'I am.'

'You worked with Jon Makokha.'

Justus gave no confirmation, but his silence was enough.

'We need men who can think like you.'

He didn't ask who was 'we'.

Makhan Singh, already known for his fierce trade unionism and multiracial advocacy, was becoming a big name among the Kenyan-Indians and native Kenyans who desperately sought change. His speeches in Nairobi began to lean harder into the language of collective action, drawing directly from the Indian anti-colonial struggle and the solidarity movements that had swept through Durban and Bombay.

Patel, the Indian clerk at Clifton & Radcliffe understood the magnitude.

'They don't know how to handle this,' Patel muttered over a teacup one evening. 'The British can't keep pretending the sun won't set. It's already fallen over India. That's why they watch Makhan Singh so closely. He knows the tides.'

Justus stirred his tea slowly. 'They still think Africa will be different. That we will wait.'

Patel scoffed. 'You've seen the courts. We are not men to them. We are labour. Transport. I've been called 'boy' long enough.'

'It won't be long and they'll make a mistake, they'll miscalculate. You'll see.' Justus said.

Patel's eyes narrowed. 'There's a file you should see. The land commissions - they're pushing new transfers.'

'You have it?'

'Not yet. But I know who does.'

Justus' work was deliberately restricted and his seniors occupied his days with legal research. The significant cases were steered elsewhere. His Indian counterparts, despite their exclusion, fought ruthlessly in the courts, drawing legal tactics from India's resistance. Trade unions tightened their grip, bolstered by Indian and African workers who had begun to see themselves as aligned.

He sat at his desk, buried beneath stacks of legal documents and case files, when Patel came in unnoticed and put a file before him. He placed it on the desk as if it were something fragile or dangerous.

'I've been watching the files they send to the senior partners,' Patel whispered. 'There's one I wasn't supposed to see.'

He gestured to the folder. 'It's what I told you. New land allocations. Quiet transfers. Names you wouldn't expect. They're moving properties, some already occupied by African families, into the hands of colonial loyalists. It's not just the Highlands anymore. They're creeping into Coast Province. Even parts of Nyanza. Places where resistance is starting to stir.'

Justus opened the folder, his eyes narrowing as he scanned the contents. Survey maps, lists of names, internal memos marked *urgent* and *confidential*. And there - an internal note: *Expedite due to increasing labour unrest.*

'They're trying to cripple the workers,' said Patel.

A phrase appeared repeatedly: *Facilitate immediate clearance.*

'They're setting the groundwork,' Justus muttered. 'If they push these families out, they break the base of the unions. Labourers without land have no bargaining power.'

Patel nodded grimly. 'They don't want to make the same mistake they made with India. This time, they'll try to choke this before it grows.'

His hand slid into his pocket and retrieved a small, folded piece of paper. Carefully, he placed it on the desk beside the file.

'Makhan Singh sent this for you. I was told to deliver it in person.'

Justus unfolded the note.

Tea House, Grogan Road. Friday, noon.

He studied the note. 'Why me?'

'Because you don't ask the wrong questions. And because Singh's network believes in you.'

Patel reached for the door. 'Be careful. This is not a case.'

Four days later, Justus sat in the corner of a modest tea house on Grogan Road, the folded file Patel had given him, including all new files he'd managed to secure now a regular burden in his leather satchel. Across from him, Makhan Singh sipped his chai with the composure of a man long accustomed to walking the edges of danger.

Singh's eyes, sharp behind his wire-rimmed glasses, stayed fixed on Justus. 'You've read it, I presume.'

'Every word,' Justus said, his voice steady. 'They're orchestrating a land squeeze. Quietly forcing Africans off arable land under legal technicalities - survey errors, expired leases, forced relocations disguised as development projects.'

Singh nodded. 'It's the oldest trick in the Empire's playbook. You control land, you control labour.'

'They think it will destabilize the unions.'

'They think we're blind,' Singh said, leaning forward. 'But we see them. The question is - will we act fast enough?'

Justus exhaled. 'What do you need from me?'

'The unions are fragmented,' Singh explained, his voice now low, the café's quiet hum offering them a fragile cover. 'There are pockets in Mombasa, in Kisumu, in Nairobi, but no unified front. Fred Kubai and I have spoken. It's time for an East African Trade Union Congress - a central body to unite the scattered groups.'

'And you want me to help draft it.'

'I need more than drafts, Justus. I need you to be a legal mind that structures it so they can't tear it apart in court.'

Justus hesitated.

'How dangerous will this be?' he asked carefully, thinking of Margaret.

Singh gave a faint smile. 'My friend, if you're not already living on the edge you're taking too much space.' Then more seriously, 'Dangerous enough to matter.'

Justus's fingers brushed the edge of the file still in his bag. 'When do we start?'

Singh finished his chai, rose up. 'We already have.'

Without another word, he disappeared into the street.

Chapter 7

Retaliation

Friends and family gathered to celebrate Justus and Margaret. Henry had made the journey from London with his wife, along with Jack, the one-armed cook whom Justus had befriended in Wales. Mr. Donovan stood outside the large tent speaking to Henry.

'I find this a moment of true reconciliation,' Henry was saying.

'Reconciliation?' Mr. Donovan asked.

'Why, yes, reconciliation.' Henry gulped down his beer. 'Look,' he waved his arm around at the dancing guests. 'All these international folk. In a beautiful British colony.'

But there were only four white folk in a party of over a hundred native, Indian and Pakistani Kenyans. Himself, Mr. Donovan and their wives. *Reconciliation has hardly begun*, Mr. Donovan thought.

Days before the wedding, a messenger had appeared at Justus's door carrying no envelope, just a folded sheet wrapped tightly in twine. The handwriting was familiar, though no names were written - only the words: *To our brother in the city.* They wished him peace, joy, and the kind of life they could not yet afford to dream of for themselves. *Your duty to us is fulfilled,* the letter said. *A husband has new battles, and we release you from the old ones.* There was no signature, only a final line that lingered in his chest: *See you soon, on the other side.*

Justus had folded the letter and put it in a safe place. Throughout the celebration, even as Margaret's hand rested in his, his mind drifted to the brotherhood in Mombasa - men still hunted by forces that did not know their names.

He stood talking with Jack. 'I feel as though I left them behind to rot.'

'Not so.' Jack assured him. 'Victory come wid a high cost, mi bredda.'

'At the price of others.' He said ruefully, sipping his drink.

On the edge of the tent, Mr. Donovan wiped his brow, squinting at the crowded dance floor. He turned to Henry, still clinging to their unfinished conversation.

'You really believe reconciliation is near?' Donovan asked, tipping his glass towards the jubilant crowd.

Mr. Donovan had come to Kenya with the promise of land. He was not a cruel man, but he lived in the quiet illusion that benevolence could excuse the foundations of colonial rule. He treated his workers with what he considered dignity - paid their wages, provided shelter - and prided himself on introducing modern farming methods that kept hunger at bay. To Mr. Donovan these acts of civility were proof that the settler had elevated the life of the native. He longed for reconciliation, though he imagined it as an agreement where the coloniser and the colonised coexisted under a system still tilted in the settler's favour. Despite his kind manner and genuine desire for peace, Mr. Donovan never fully grasped that true reconciliation would require the dismantling of the very privileges he quietly hoped to preserve.

Henry sighed, swirling the last of his drink. 'No, not yet. Maybe not even close. But look at them. For one night, the rules don't matter.'

Donovan frowned. 'What about tomorrow?'

Henry's smile thinned. 'Tomorrow the rules return. But they won't last forever.' Although Mr. Donovan was a bit drunk, and Henry equally, they both knew that unity once sparked was not easily extinguished. Around them were Kenyans from all walks of life. Various tribes of native Kenyans, Indians and Pakistanis.

Henry knew that the power of unity within Kenya would soon see the country to its independence.

Weeks after his wedding, Justus was invited to a meeting by Singh. Months had passed since their first meeting. He slid into the seat opposite Singh, his satchel heavier than it had been months before.

'You've done the revisions?'

Justus handed him the thin sheaf of papers. The draft constitution for the East African Trade Union Congress. He had gone through it to ensure no loose ends.

'They'll fight it,' Justus said. 'They'll try to bury the registration under procedural delays. Force you to rewrite until you make a mistake.'

Singh skimmed the pages, lingering on the critical clauses. 'See? Your job is to anticipate what's ahead of us.'

'You'll also need a legal strategy for when the police come,' Justus added. 'They'll accuse you of inciting unrest. Of sedition.'

'They always accuse us of something.'

'You'll need formal protection for assets too. When they can't break you, they'll come for the money, anything tied to you.'

Singh opened his briefcase, put the papers in carefully. 'We have a strong network that will ensure the Congress survives.'

Justus studied him. The colonial system had a tempo: watch, delay, arrest, erase. He knew that Singh knew it better than most. Across the table, Singh's eyes hardened. 'This isn't just another union, my friend. It is a structure that can hold long after men like me are gone. You understand that.'

The vision for the East Africa Trade Union Congress was broad, but without structure it would fracture under the pressure the colonial system was already beginning to apply. It needed law as both shield and weapon. By late 1948, the Union Congress was no longer just a draft.

The colonial administration didn't miss the movement's quiet making. They had become aware of efforts to establish the Congress although formal registration was still pending. Singh and Fred were affiliated with people that mattered including Bildad Kaggia and

Jomo Kenyatta, who was now steering the Kenya African Union. Justus was confident that the support of such people would see through the legal recognition of EATUC.

Since its founding in 1944, KAU had grown as the political mouthpiece for African grievances, but its reach didn't yet extend deep into labour. That was to be the domain of EATUC - labour, strikes, pressure points the colonial state feared more than speeches.

By early 1949, the East African Trade Union Congress had taken shape. Makhan Singh and Fred Kubai had done the impossible: they had built a cross-racial, cross-regional alliance in a colony where such collaboration was both feared and forbidden. But the colonial government would not let the Congress stand.

Within weeks of the EATUC's formal application for registration, the colonial Labour Department struck back: *Irresponsible. Political. Subversive.*

In elite clubs white men clutched gin and talked about communist infiltration. Their fear was not misplaced. There was an undeniable local hunger for freedom, however that freedom came. What terrified the colonial authority was not so much Moscow and Soviet-inspired communism as it was the collaboration of groups within Kenya.

The British colonial authority's response was swift. They denied the EATUC's registration outright, branding it illegal. Surveillance intensified. Files on Singh and Kubai thickened. By mid-year 1949, plans were discussed to deport Makhan Singh back to India. But India being a free country did not give them the liberty to move people. There was no law, no precedent that could justify removing Singh.

Into this storm walked Pio Gama Pinto who had just returned from India, stepping off the ship to a Kenya bristling with contradictions. The hands of the empire gripped the levers of power tighter than ever. Pinto was a journalist and political organiser. He was no stranger to colonial harassment, and his editorials and underground bulletins became razor-sharp instruments, cutting through the official propaganda.

'*Singh and Kubai have shown us what a union can be,*' Justus wrote to Pinto weeks after his return to Kenya. '*A voice for all - Indian, African, Arab. They challenge the very foundations of imperial control. Can you help??*'

Towards the end of the year, Patel walked into Justus' office and handed him a letter. Pinto had written briefly, '*The colonial administration fears not their methods, but their success. They fear unity. Let us meet.*'

Meanwhile the colonial police raided presses, seized pamphlets, and harassed newsboys on street corners, but Pinto's articles were read widely, passed from worker to worker, from office to marketplace.

Justus met Pinto one afternoon at a small café near the Khoja Mosque, at a shaded corner.

'Makhan's becoming a ghost in their files,' Pinto said. 'They'll try to crush the people around him.' He sipped his tea, looking at Justus over the rim of his cup. 'They'll be watching you too,' he said matter of factly. 'They might even think you're the architect, if they find out that you had anything to do with the draft. I suggest you keep a low profile.'

'I can't pull away when I am needed the most,' Justus began.

Pinto's mouth twitched, somewhere between a smirk and concern. 'Bravery and recklessness have thin borders.'

'If I vanish - '

Pinto's expression hardened. 'Even though they've decided EATUC must collapse, we will not give up. The refusal to register was their opening move. Their typical second move would be to go after the smaller unions. To break them one by one. But it will not happen.'

'I was hoping you would push through for the registration of the Congress.'

'I will do what I do best.' Pinto tapped his notebook. 'They need to see that the world is watching. When the real fight begins, the unions will hold the line.'

Justus stood up, and so did Pinto. The two men shook hands.

'Keep the pressure public,' Justus tipped his hat and left.

The weeks that followed were tense. Pinto's articles stirred the streets. He documented Singh's defiance and Kubai's relentless efforts and speeches. He named the colonial hypocrisy, called out their manufactured panic, and exposed their manipulation of the legal system.

As 1949 closed, the government tightened its net. The efforts to suppress the Congress heated. The leaders were marked, their movements tracked.

Chapter 8

The Arrests of 1950

The clatter of metal pots and the faint shuffle of Margaret's slippers in the kitchen drifted through the open door as Justus sat by the radio, his tie hanging loose around his neck. The morning news from the Kenya Broadcasting Service crackled through the small wooden box.

"Breaking news this morning: prominent trade union leaders Fred Kubai and Makhan Singh were arrested earlier today by colonial authorities on charges relating to subversive activities and the incitement of industrial unrest."

Justus slowly tightened his tie. The broadcaster continued, laced with the colonial government's carefully written script: *'agitators', 'communist sympathies'*.

He switched to the Kikuyu station, which was often filtered but sometimes if you listened closely, you caught what the government missed. Radio was a powerful means of controlling information, therefore downplaying the significance of certain events such as arrests and presenting them as routine law enforcement. During the late 1940s and early 1950s, particularly as anti-colonial resistance grew, the authorities filtered, delayed, or spun news content to align with colonial interests. Important details were often omitted or twisted compared to the more straightforward reporting in the English-language radio or print media, in order to minimise their significance or frame them as threats to public order.

When he pulled up near his office, Justus bought the Daily Chronicle from a street seller.

TRADE UNIONISTS ARRESTED. COLONIAL POLICE MOVE TO STAMP OUT RADICAL NETWORKS.

Inside his office, a newspaper was already spread open on his desk like a battle map, the black ink looking fresh. His secretary, Asha, entered with his morning coffee.

'They've taken him,' she whispered, her voice tight. 'Singh.'

'Yes, and Fred.' Justus said with disdain.

Her family had admired Singh for years. Justus could see the raw fear sitting behind her eyes.

'They can't deport him,' He said to reassure her.

'No,' Asha agreed, clearing her throat, then with a stronger voice, 'But they can silence him.'

She edged closer, now lowering her voice. 'Someone from the administration's office came asking about you,' she said. 'Asking who you meet. I told them I only bring you coffee.'

Justus stared at the headline again. 'Thank you, Asha,' he said. He put the paper aside.

That night just before they went to bed, they heard a soft knock. Three taps. Two more.

Justus unlatched the door to find a young man, with a folded note clutched tightly in his hand.

"Salim sent me," he said and hurried away.

He closed the door, unfolding the note. *They've scattered us. I may go north. stay alive. Protect what matters.*

He knew where the *north* was. And it wasn't north of anywhere. It was underground.

One afternoon in December, Justus sat alone on a park bench off Government Road, a brief escape from the walls of his office, his jacket across his lap. He listened to the city. Newspapers still ran stories of progress and order. But he listened to the street hawkers, the cautious complaints floating from market stalls. These were the real headlines.

Pio Gama Pinto had covered the *Nairobi General Strike* that followed the arrests of Fred Kubai and Makhan Singh back in May.

He also wrote a pointed piece in the *Daily Chronicle* responding to the colonial authorities' refusal to register the East African Trade Union Congress (EATUC) and their attempts to deport Makhan Singh. Pinto lauded Singh's leadership, criticized the administration's actions as 'a cowardly retreat from justice,' and called for pan-community solidarity, directly challenging colonial policy.

Amid the noise of the city, Justus could hear Pinto's warning: *They'll be watching you too.*

Chapter 9

Crossroads

Justus was awed by the coordination and resilience of individuals who were willing to risk everything for the cause they believed in. Resistance activity and political activism heightened after the arrests of Fred Kubai and Makhan Singh. Mau Mau fighters and urban political leaders began to take stronger ground. Jomo Kenyatta continued to publicly promote peaceful negotiation and constitutional reform, but he too was being closely monitored.

One rainy day in July 1951, a letter arrived from London, bearing Jack's familiar handwriting. Jack's cheerful message relayed the news that he had taken up his father's old job at the officer's household and that he was soon to receive a fake arm.

"Mi bredda Justus," the letter started. *"London still cold like a taxman heart, mi bredda. But guess wha? Mi step inna di ol' man shoes now - pick up him job at di officer dem house. Can yuh believe it? Mi deh yah a serve tea to di same kind o' man who near drop bomb pon mi head. Life funny so, eh? And hear dis now - dem a build mi one proper new wooden arm. Dem say it can bend an' move proper! Maybe next time mi can finally gimme yuh a proper shake wid mi right hand. If di arm play nice, mi might even train it fi write sweet love letter dem, save mi di headache, yuh know?"*

Justus chuckled at Jack's witty remarks. In his reply, he talked about his own transformations, and the goings on in the country, careful not to reveal detail in case the letter fell in the wrong hands. He was glad to hear Jack was settling in well in his new job in London, and promised to make his way across the waters to see him, when things quietened down in Kenya. Justus envisioned them, sharing a good pot of tea, and talking about all the roads they'd travelled since the old days in Wales.

Towards the end of the year he received a letter from Henry, who followed the goings on in East Africa and even more closely in Kenya. He passionately wrote about his belief that all people, regardless of their skin colour, were equal, and that the white coloniser was no greater than the colonised. He expressed his conviction that their intertwined destinies demanded cooperation, and hoped that someday their paths would cross again.

It was a quiet evening in Nairobi, and the dying embers of the fire crackled in the living room of Justus's home. Justus's father, Muriuki, had come to visit them, and they now sat in the dimly lit room. Muriuki was against Justus's involvement of any kind in the uprising groups that claimed to fight for Kenya's independence.

As Muriuki rose to tend to the fading flames, Justus stopped him with a weary gesture. 'Let's leave it,' he said, his voice tinged with exhaustion. 'It's late, and I have an early day tomorrow.'

Muriuki, a wise and weathered man, shook his head gently. He lifted a finger and made a familiar gesture. 'You are not a teenager, Justus,' he said, his voice filled with paternal concern. 'You have a wife and two children. These *land and freedom armies*, you must not engage with them.'

Justus couldn't suppress the turmoil within him. He paced the room, his frustration palpable. 'Father, why didn't you fight back?'

Muriuki's countenance was filled with sadness. 'We couldn't.'

The flickering light from the fire cast shadows on their faces, accentuating the lines of age on his father's face. Muriuki had endured much in his lifetime but was a man with a calm and measured demeanour. Justus often thought about his father's generation - those who had first seen the colonial flags rise over their homelands, who had watched railways carve through their fields, and who had heard a foreign tongue dictating unfamiliar laws. There had been skirmishes, refusals, defiance. But the empire was a storm greater than their resources or their networks could withstand. It had pressed down with military force, land alienation, heavy taxation, and the systematic erasure of indigenous authority.

By the 1920s and 30s, many of Justus's father's peers had been beaten into tired submission. Many chose survival over endless struggle. Others were coerced, given small positions of land under colonial rule in exchange for loyalty.

'We did not give up because we were weak,' Muriuki said.

Justus had not inherited his father's ability to let go. He was fiercely resolute and driven by a desire for justice.

That night, after his conversation with his father, Justus lay in bed, his thoughts racing. He could choose to live in peace alongside his superiors, hoping for independence to arrive in his lifetime. Or he could take a stand for people like his father, mother, and brothers who had never been heard. And for his sons, who deserved to live in an independent country. But the fight for independence came with immense risks and uncertainties. It meant putting his family in jeopardy and potentially sacrificing the comfortable life he had built for them. As he lay in the darkness, Justus knew that a pivotal decision needed to be made.

Chapter 10

The Inheritance

The Kenyan struggle for independence was beginning to catch ground in many areas around the country. It was 1957 and many men involved in uprisings were being tracked down and just as many were joining the movement for independence. Justus, who now worked as a lecturer in Egerton Farm School, followed these events closely. He taught basic subjects - science, mathematics, and English to a new generation of African students. The shift from activist lawyer to educator was a big change, but Justus saw it as a chance to contribute quietly to the country's future. In the college's classrooms and agricultural fields, he found a different kind of resistance: nurturing knowledge and skills that might one day help transform the land.

Justus made his way to his lecture hall, his afro now trimmed short, and his idealistic zeal mellowed into a thoughtful wisdom. Responsibilities of fatherhood had a way of calming even the rebellious fervour, and his father had been right in trying to calm him. His twin boys, Timotheo and Michael were growing fast and their future was on his mind every day.

Justus watched as his students, faces eager and hopeful, filed into the lecture hall. Although this was an agricultural college, he had been permitted to give a lecture on African and British History, and as he watched the crowded hall, he felt a sense of responsibility towards his students.

Outside the walls of the college, Kenya was changing fast. The movement for independence was gaining momentum, and the government's crackdown on freedom fighters was intensifying. He followed the news closely, balancing his role as an educator with his memories of the days when he'd have jumped full in. As he walked from the lecture hall, Justus overheard hushed conversations in the corridors about the latest arrests, the daring acts of sabotage against colonial infrastructure, and the passionate speeches of leaders like Jomo Kenyatta and Dedan Kimathi.

A young man with a determined look in his eyes, approached him. 'Sir,' he asked, 'Do you think the Mau Mau uprising will lead us to independence?'

Justus paused, considering his response carefully. 'The Mau Mau uprising reflects the desperation and frustration of our long-term oppression. But it's essential to remember that change can come through various means - through peaceful negotiations, and education. Each of us must decide where we can make the most significant impact.'

Justus watched the student walk away. That evening, he sat at the dinner table with his wife and sons, his thoughts racing. His boys, oblivious of any political unrest, roared with innocent laughter and energy, Margaret captivated by their charm, laughing along. The struggle for independence would shape the world they would inherit.

As the night settled in, their neighbour, Njoroge knocked on the door and Margaret let him in.

They stood by the window. 'There have been talks.' Njoroge began. He was a worker at the college. They walked out to sit at the porch of Justus' house, overlooking the cornfield. Justus settled the lantern on a hook. It had been three years since he moved his family to Njoro.

'There's a group in Murang'a. Intelligent young men.'

'They are not organised, Njoroge.' Then after a short pause, 'I cannot be involved,' he said firmly. 'I have two boys to raise.'

'I have more, my friend.' Njoroge went and sat down. 'We must do something, or we shall have nothing by the end of this.'

'How long has it been.' Justus muttered, to no one in particular. He was thinking of those years in Mombasa. They were sure that they would bring Kenya to independence. Then almost a decade in Nairobi. He walked back and sat down.

'Independence will come, sooner or later.' He said.

When Macharia Kimemia, leader of Mau Mau operations in Aberdare was killed, along with ten followers in a battle near Nairobi that year, many more men joined the uprising.

Muriuki died later that year. Women wailed, their cries rising with the morning mist, expressing their grief. Relatives gathered from near and far, sitting together in the homestead, sharing stories of his life. A goat was slaughtered as part of the ritual and Justus, his brothers and others who handled the deceased washed with its undigested food. They shaved their heads and slept in the bush for a day to restore peace, following the taboo *thahu* of handling the deceased. The cottage felt vacant, even with the multitude of grievers. His mother had died some years back.

Mr. Donovan did something uncommon. He declared Justus' owner of an acre of the land where his parents had been labourers since his birth. 'On this land,' Mr. Donovan wrote, 'You may bury your Father.' And at the end of the certificate, he wrote, 'Muriuki was a fine man.'

Not surprisingly, Mr. and Mrs. Donovan attended the funeral ceremony. A fence was put up to divide the small portion of land assigned to Justus from the rest of the land.

'We appreciate everything you did for my parents.'

'They did a lot for us too.'

Justus looked down at the locked hands, his and Mr. Donovan's. Mrs. Donovan, whose name he had never learned, stood tear-faced close by. She was small and frail. He looked back at Mr. Donovan, thinking, *I did grow up in the land of my inheritance.* He smiled, 'Thank you very much, sir.'

Muriuki's passing had left a veil over Justus' home. As Justus and Margaret sat together one evening, Margaret could sense the turmoil in her husband's heart. Justus gazed at a family portrait that hung on the wall. 'I'm thinking of going back to college.' Margaret's eyebrows arched in surprise. 'What for? You love what you do.'

Justus looked at her, 'I'm tired of standing on the sidelines, Margaret. I've distanced myself from the fight for independence, to protect you and the boys. Yet now, with my own father gone, I can't help but feel the responsibility to put things right. For our sons. Can you understand?'

Margaret nodded slowly, although not fully understanding. Justus added, 'Kenya needs to gain its independence. And maybe I can contribute by shaping the minds of young leaders who will lead our nation towards freedom.'

'Your father would have been proud of you for choosing a peaceful way to fight for independence.'

Justus managed a small smile. 'Even a peaceful way won't be easy, and it means I will need to study in India or London, but it's a path I feel compelled to take.'

Margaret snuggled close. 'Then take it.' Justus placed an arm around her, feeling a renewed sense of purpose.

Chapter 11

The wake of Independence

Justus's eyes fixed on the bold headline: *"Tom Mboya tables the motion 'no confidence' in the colonial government, arguing that the colonial masters had failed to improve the status of Africans."* It was 1958, and the cry for change was sweeping through Kenya like a wildfire.

He had returned home earlier from England after ten months of studies, after receiving an invitation to teach at the Royal Technical College of East Africa, where he would be teaching Economics. He saw it as an opportunity to be a part of the evolving history of Kenya.

Margaret walked into the room with a tray of steaming milky Kenyan tea in her hand. Her eyes met his. She set his cup of tea before him and sat beside him. 'We need to move away from here anyway. It is no longer safe for the boys.'

There were many deaths during the past year. Innocent villagers had fallen victim to the violence that swept through the country.

'You're right. We need to move from here,' Justus conceded. He took his tea, sipping it slowly as he mulled over his thoughts. 'I used to think independence would have found my boys still in their cradles.'

'There's not a better time for independence than now.' Margaret said firmly.

Justus drank the rest of his tea. He would take the job and move his family back to Nairobi. The city held promise and uncertainty in equal measure, but he was willing to embrace both.

PART 2

The End of an Era

2002-2003

Chapter 12

Pappi's Awakening

It was March 2002. Pappi strolled along the streets of London. At 54 she was poised, her short, salt-and-pepper hair framing a face set with determination. For the first time in a year, she had gone shopping for clothes, a necessary indulgence, prompted by the upcoming firm party. The extension of their house to accommodate Elizabeth's family had drained her finances and she'd found good reason to tighten her spending, not that she would have had it any other way. They lived in a large three storey house, each maintaining their part of the house although Pappi constantly intruded into their space, doing this or that. With her grandchildren growing and needing their own rooms, she had offered to cover the costs of extension. The last thing she wanted was for them to begin searching for a bigger home to move to.

She was emerging out of a clothes store on Bond Street on this cloudy Tuesday when something caught her eye - a bold headline on a stack of newspapers at a nearby vendor's stand: *"Kenyans Strive for a New President."* The words stirred feelings long forgotten, memories of the country of her birth began to rise within her.

She hurried over and bought a copy. *"With elections looming, Kenyans voice hope for change after decades of autocratic rule. Full story, page 4."*

She flipped quickly to the article which spoke of mounting pressure for democratic reform, of a younger generation demanding new leadership, and of a country at the threshold of a new political era. The longing for a fresh start felt achingly familiar. She had left Kenya during a time of personal turmoil, a decade after independence. She remembered those early years after independence, the upheaval of change everywhere.

Pappi worked as a criminal lawyer and had built a strong reputation for always standing firmly on the side of justice. She had handled countless high-profile cases, among them the Barrington case which dragged on for seven years. Her mastery of the courtroom and ability to navigate the most complex corners of criminal law made her widely respected in legal circles. Her life had been defined by precision and certainty. Yet the news of Kenya's political evolution unsettled something within her. She wondered if it was time to revisit her roots, a thought she'd shelved away a long time ago.

She hurried along to her lunch with a colleague. Soft murmurs of conversation, the clink of cutlery, and the faint scent of freshly baked bread welcomed her as she entered The Wolseley. Lotte was seated at a corner table.

'Punctual as ever,' She greeted. 'You look thoughtful. Something on your mind?'

Pappi sat down. 'I came across an article about Kenya. It's stirring up more than I expected.'

Lotte raised an eyebrow. 'Hmm. You haven't been back for years, have you?'

'More than Two decades,' Pappi admitted. 'But this - there's talk of real change. New leadership. It's hard to ignore.'

Lotte leaned back, swirling her glass of white wine. 'Change is always seductive. Especially when you feel settled. But of course you're not thinking of it seriously.'

'That's what makes it complicated,' Pappi mumbled. 'This news unsettles me.'

'Like you left something important behind.' Lotte said with a sudden far-away look. She had fled Bosnia in the early nineties with her mother and young daughter, leaving behind the rubble of a life shattered by the Balkan War. Lotte's husband had arranged the documents and the safe passage, with plans to follow within weeks. But the war closed in faster than they had imagined, and he never made it out.

A waiter appeared, ready to take their order. Pappi put her hand on Lotte's. 'Hey, let's enjoy lunch and talk about what we're wearing to the party on Saturday.' The conversation drifted to lighter topics, the upcoming firm's party pulling their thoughts away from the past.

Chapter 13

Through the eyes of a child

There was a blend of cultures in Kenya in the mid 1950s - indigenous ethnic groups, Indians, Goans, Pakistanis and British colonials. One sunny morning in Nakuru, the market streets were alive with activity. Pappi walked hand in hand with her parents, relishing the sight of many faces. The locals, familiar with the family, greeted them warmly.

'Good morning, Reverend and Mrs. Salmon!' called out Mama Njeri, a vendor selling colourful fabrics. 'Would you like to see the latest fabrics for your sewing, ma'am?'

Pappi's mother smiled warmly as she examined the fabrics. Mrs. Brunton, one of their neighbours, was also there, examining fabric. 'We might need some for Pappi's clothing, now that she's grown out of most of her clothes.'

Mrs Brunton investigated Pappi with her eyes. 'Yes, she'll need a new dress.' She decided. 'My Jessica is the same. The girl is up to the roof. Nothing will fit her.' Pappi looked down at her blue dress, slightly above her knees. She didn't think it needed to be longer than that.

As she stood by her mother, Pappi caught sight of Lady Thompson, known for her keen eye for high-fashion. With her dresses and air of importance, Lady Thompson was a striking figure. Pappi had seen her picture in magazines in Mary-Anne's home, and once at Tony's mother's tea party engaging in leisurely conversations with other guests. She wondered what it felt like to be a lady.

'Lady Thompson, have you heard about the upcoming gathering at the club?' Mrs. Brunton inquired as they crossed paths.

Lady Thompson nodded, her voice tinged with excitement. 'Indeed I have! A splendid affair. Do bring your family along. It promises to be quite the social event.'

Pappi observed how the women conversed, their voices animated. Their faces alight with enthusiasm. She had often heard stories of their gatherings at the club, where tea and gossip flowed freely. Mary-Anne's mother was a frequent guest at those parties, and on such nights the girls were allowed to have sleepovers either at Pappi's or Mary-Anne's. Pappi's own parents had no place in that world. Their lives circled the church and its community, not the glittering rooms of the social elite. What Pappi knew of such affairs came mostly from the sidelines, through borrowed glimpses and observations in other people's homes.

As they continued their stroll through the market, Pappi saw Mary, who worked for the former Lieutenant Colonel McCarthy. She stood with the Colonel's wife, adjusting her mistress's hat with utmost care. Her mistress was rarely seen in public. It was rumoured that she'd developed a condition that left her vulnerable to the sun, but that she had refused to return to England where the danger of the sun was obviously deemed less.

'Mary, do be careful with the hat,' Mrs. McCarthy admonished. Mary nodded, her expression deferential. 'Of course, Madam.'

Pappi's young mind absorbed the dynamics of life at the market place - the colonial women who enjoyed their privileges and the Kenyan locals who made those privileges possible. It was a world of contrasts. Yet as they concluded their shopping, Pappi felt the warm embrace of the Rift Valley community. Strangely, very strangely even to a child of eight, it was a life where everyone seemed to know their place.

Chapter 14

Roots

Two weeks had passed since she had stumbled upon that newspaper article about Kenya. Her thoughts had been consumed by the country she left, ever since. She found herself reminiscing about old friends, even those with whom she had lost touch over the years. Her mind repeatedly returned to the political scenery in Kenya, a place she hadn't called home in many years, yet a place that had always remained a part of her.

Pappi was pacing her spacious living room, repositioning things as she often did when lost in thought. She knew, as if it were an unshakable truth, that she had to return to Kenya.

'It's strange how sometimes you just know that you know something,' she mused aloud to herself. She had raised her daughter Elizabeth and enjoyed the luxuries of her affluent life. As she stood in her rearranged living room, gazing out at the London skyline through her large windows, Pappi knew that her path was clear.

President Moi's early years in office were marked by relative stability and efforts to promote national unity. However, over time, his rule also witnessed the rise of tribal tensions and deepening political divisions that would leave a lasting impact on the nation. The unresolved fractures of that era stirred a quiet urgency within Pappi. She especially felt a deep concern for those whose voices could not be heard because of their under-privileged positions, cut off from education because of a corrupt regime. During the last two weeks she had read everything she could find on the marginalised and vulnerable in Kenya, who bore the brunt of the difficulties, lacking basic healthcare and proper living conditions.

'Addressing these issues is crucial for Kenya's future,' She was saying to Mary-Anne, her voice filled with conviction. She had been on the phone constantly in the past week, mostly with Mary-Anne and Chris. Mary-Anne knew little about politics and her ideas were often wildly impractical, but she was inspiring to talk to. It was striking how, in some ways, she thought like her mother. Pappi didn't think that she ever saw Kenya as a country, as England or France. But she had a heart of gold and felt terribly much for the less privileged.

Pappi leaned back in her chair, her phone pressed to her ear, as she continued her conversation with Mary-Anne. Even if some of her ideas seemed wildly out of place, Mary-Anne was a comfort to talk to.

'What I mean,' She was saying, 'is that with all things considered, there is more room elsewhere in the country than crowded places in Nairobi. Think of the north and the coastal hinterlands. Or even some of the eastern parts.'

Pappi smiled. Mary-Anne's bold suggestion for a project to relocate slum residents into newly built housing in less populated regions of Kenya was undeniably appealing - though her understanding of the complex social dynamics involved remained limited.

'It's a bold idea, and not that simple.'

Mary-Anne's voice held a hint of disappointment, but she remained undeterred. 'I know, but if you want to do this, nothing can stop you. Look at your decision to leave everything you know and move to a country that is as much a stranger to you as China is!'

She laughed. 'I haven't left yet.' She admired Mary-Anne's optimism. 'Wait. Kenya is no stranger to me!' Pappi cried defensively.

'Well, in that case it's no stranger to me too.'

After a moment of quiet the two women laughed.

'How long has it been now?' Pappi asked.

'Oh I lost count. Too many decades.'

Chris was a steadying influence for Pappi. He did not fully understand why she particularly felt the urge to be part of a country she left many years ago at this stage in her life, but he supported her. She told him about Mary-Anne's intriguing idea the previous night. He laughed and said he thought it was overambitious.

"Exactly what I had said to Mary-Anne." she answered. And, in his typically measured way, he had said, "If you're ever going to consider development work, Paps, the first thing you need to do is understand the true cost. Dreams may not cost, but real work demands careful planning."

Chapter 15

Reflections

Late May brought a comforting warmth to the small garden in Chris's backyard. A gentle breeze rustled the leaves of the old oak tree. Chris, dressed in a plain t-shirt and a pair of shorts, sat on his weathered bench, mulling over Pappi's plan to return to Kenya.

He was born in the Rift Valley. His grandfather moved to Kenya in 1897, two years after the British Empire established the East Africa Protectorate. When Chris's grandfather arrived in East Africa the region was raw, and to the eyes of the British Empire, ripe for organization. The Uganda Railway, later called the Kenya-Uganda Railway, was pushing inwards from Mombasa to Port Florence, and Chris's grandfather was among the officers sent to oversee administration and secure the Empire's interests.

In the early 1900s life in the protectorate was arduous. Days were long and filled with the work of taming the African wilderness. They laid railway tracks across unforgiving terrain, where, in 1898 near Tsavo, two lions terrorised and killed dozens of Indian workers brought in by the British to build the Uganda Railway. Despite this, Sir Charles Eliot actively encouraged European settlement. And so settlements sprouted, even near railway depots, beginning the gradual European colonization of the interior.

Chris's grandfather was stationed in what later became part of the Rift Valley Province. These White Highlands were ideal regions for British farmers because of their temperate climate and rich soils and they became the prize. British officers and settlers viewed it as a slice of Europe transplanted into Africa.

Chris's father was the second generation of white Kenyans who called the country home. He was educated in a school for settler children, and later became a doctor, travelling between estates, treating children and farmhands alike.

Life in the Rift Valley offered privilege and isolation. But there was always the undercurrent of tension. Indigenous communities, increasingly marginalized and displaced, were never entirely silent.

By the time Chris came along in late 1946, the Empire was no longer invincible. The sight of a black girl in a school for white children did not seem too odd to him. His father had talked about her - the abandoned little girl who'd spent her first weeks in his care. Pappi had been the only black student at their local missionary school, and for a long time he had watched her endure the ridicule and isolation. Chris did not care much for school, and would have been happier exploring the mountains of Central Kenya. His and Pappi's friendship had been forged through the shared experience of not fitting in.

Today, as Pappi spoke endlessly about her plan to return to Kenya, Chris worried for her safety and the challenges she might face in a country that had seen its fair share of turmoil.

He sighed, walking into the house, poured himself a drink, and walked back outside. He remembered after his sixteenth birthday, the conflict of whether to leave Kenya or to stay. Pappi chose to remain behind, the last of their circle of friends to leave the country. She had been determined to carve her own path in a society that was shedding its colonial past rapidly.

Then one night in 1972, Pappi's voice trembled over the line, her words choking with emotion as she shared her news. She was pregnant and alone. Chris remembered feeling her despair through the receiver.

Chapter 16

A letter from the Past

While Elizabeth had no memories of her early years in Kenya, the stories her mother had shared with her painted a vivid picture of what it must have been like in the first two years of her life.

She handed her mother a letter and then stood, looking at her reaction. Pappi knew it was from Timotheo before she opened it. 'Sit down Elizabeth,' she commanded, her gaze lingering on the envelope. Elizabeth resumed her seat at the kitchen table, where they were having breakfast. Jason looked up from the bills.

'What is it?' He asked, his brow furrowing with curiosity. He saw the stamp on the envelope that Pappi held, and he put down his bills. 'It's Tim, isn't it.'

'Yes, I believe so.' Pappi opened the envelope, pulling her chair back and standing, 'Excuse me. I must be alone for a moment.' She went to the study, walked to the window as she pulled out the contents from the envelope.

He had received her letter, he said, and was sorry to reply so late.

Njoki is eager to see you. We are all overjoyed at the thought of seeing you again. Rosina was here just yesterday, and she has been talking about you non-stop since we received your letter.

Memories of Timotheo and Njoki flooded her mind. During those bleak years before she had packed up her daughter and moved to England, these were some of the few people that had stood by her. She looked back at the letter in her hand. It somehow consoled her that Timotheo's handwriting had never changed. Slanting, difficult to read. She remembered telling him to work on it in 1970, when he had written to her from the US. He had said he would not need to work on it, since he and Michael had bought a typewriter and would be bringing it home. She smiled at the memory.

Pappi had met Timotheo first, on the day before their farewell party. Professor Justus Muriuki had just finished speaking to the student union group. As the crowd began to disperse, she huddled with a group of friends, waiting for a chance to speak with him. But the secretary had come to inform them that the professor had no time to see them. As they left the building, a student shouted, 'Wait!' The professor had invited the entire student union for his sons' farewell party the following day. Professor Muriuki was famously known for random invites to events that students would otherwise never set foot in.

That was five years after Kenya's hard-won independence. The Kenya that Justus and his peers had dreamed of during the years of resistance was very slow in emerging. The aftertaste of colonial rule still lingered - in the legal system, in the social hierarchies, and in the unequal access to opportunity. Land redistribution remained a sharp point of contention and, although the Kenya African Democratic Union had dissolved itself in 1964, merging with Kenya African National Union, there were underlying political divisions.

Justus was not blind to these tensions and was respected for his criticism and his ability to speak truth without burning bridges. He told his students: *Politics is not for the distant man in the suit, but for everyone; for the people who stand in the rain waiting for buses that may never come.*

He encouraged debate, even disagreement, believing that questioning was a form of patriotism. It was not unusual for Justus to host evening gatherings at his home, where conversations about Pan-Africanism, governance, and identity stretched deep into the night. Pappi became a constant attendee to many such evenings. She remembered being intrigued by his persistent sense of motion. Justus believed that although the fight was over, it had simply changed form. Kenya was still becoming.

Now she wondered how Michael was doing. Timotheo did not mention him, nor his family. It had remained that way. She could feel an agitation building up. Dreading the thought of crying, she swallowed and went on reading.

'Ma,' Startled, Pappi turned to find Elizabeth standing beside her. 'How is Uncle Tim?'

'Fine.' She smiled, 'Just fine.' She handed Elizabeth the letter.

There wasn't anything she had kept secret from Elizabeth. They had talked about the past since she had been old enough to understand.

As Pappi walked back to rejoin Jason, she remembered the professor's words in the last event she attended: *Freedom is not a destination. It is a long road. We have taken the first step, but if we sleep now, we will find ourselves in chains of our own making.*

She had wondered then what on earth he meant.

Chapter 17

Unsettlement

'Pappi, you're faster than any of the boys!'

The girls were clambering up a tree. It was 1957, and they were 10 years old. Pappi grinned, her spirit as wild as the breeze rustling through the leaves. 'They can't catch me! I'm Pappi the tree-climbing queen!'

'You're Papillote Rafaella Salmon!' Yelled Chris from the base of the tree, cupping his mouth with his dusty hands. Several children stood around the tree looking up with their mouths open.

'Stop!' Cried Pappi.

In the mid and late 1950s many British families still lived in a state of permanence. Kenya, the jewel of East Africa, was simply home. Horse races and lawn parties carried on, in an air of colonial civility amidst the unrest in the country that somehow felt far away.

Pappi's parents, stationed in the Rift Valley by the Kenyan Alliance of Protestant Missions, were part of this world, though they occupied a slightly different social standing. She was born in September 1947, to a mother who had, for reasons unknown, abandoned her shortly after birth. She'd been a few days old when she was found abandoned in the Salmon's barn. Despite exhaustive searches throughout the region for her birth mother or any relatives, no one had come forward to claim her.

"We searched and searched,' Her father had always said.

'And mark you, it was not difficult in those days to know when a girl was pregnant out of wedlock. But to our great amazement no one had seen a pregnant girl without a husband in any village around. No one claimed you, dear child.' Her mother usually finished.

In a society where racial hierarchies were deeply ingrained, raising a black child as their own was both an act of compassion and quiet rebellion.

In the 50s the Kenyan population, especially among the Kikuyu, was increasingly resentful of the inequalities that denied them land ownership, political representation, and basic freedoms. But this news was brought to British homes mainly through newspapers like The East African Standard, which often reassured them of the colony's security, reminding them of the power of the British empire. While aware of occasional murmurs of dissatisfaction, these were largely dismissed as manageable disruptions.

One of those disruptions was Jomo Kenyatta, a name that would soon dominate both local and international headlines. He rose to prominence as a leader of the Kenya African Union, causing a mix of disdain and fear among many settler households. Radio reports from the Kenya Broadcasting Service began relaying frequent disturbances in the early 1950s, of strikes and boycotts. But when Jomo Kenyatta was detained in October 1952, shortly after the British colonial government declared a State of Emergency, many British families felt the empire was in control.

Sir Evelyn Baring, the Governor of Kenya, became a central figure, frequently featured in news bulletins and public statements assuring settlers of the administration's grip on the situation. British soldiers and loyalist African forces carried out sweeping counter-insurgency operations. Mass detentions were instituted, with thousands of people rounded up and sent to detention camps. Among the British settler community, this period hardened attitudes. Defensiveness took root. Parents still organized garden parties, children still played cricket, and on Sundays families gathered at church.

Pappi learned early on that she was different - a black girl navigating spaces where she often stood out - and she quickly grasped that not everyone would welcome her. Bullies came with the territory, but she learned not to cower. Her father taught her how to stand her ground. But her upbringing in the White Highlands, surrounded by colonial privilege and far removed from the pulse of the villages, left her cut off from her Kenyan roots.

With her childhood friends she revelled in the simple joys of life: music echoing through the valley during birthdays and any excuse they found to party. Pappi's barn was a popular hangout, especially because most weekends her parents would be gone visiting congregations in different parts of the country. And if Pappi had won anyone's heart, it was the servants in her household. They not only allowed mass sleepovers but also provided feastlike Kenyan dishes for night parties.

As they grew older, their adventures took them farther afield. They organised explorations to the mountains and valleys, from Lake Nakuru, through the ancient ruins of Hyrax Hill, past the volcanic depths of Menengai Crater, and onward to the rim of Mount Longonot.

Yet it was not all adventure; there were moments of reflection. One starry night, gathered around a campfire, they shared stories about their dreams for the future. There were seven of them, now teenagers. It was 1960, and they knew it wouldn't be long before British colonies became independent countries. The only ones seemingly unaware were their mothers, bound to their estates and reassured by imperial news that all was well. They placed their trust in their capable husbands who managed the colonies, believing the empire's hold remained firm.

Many settler's wives were shielded from the full reality of local resistance. They relied on filtered reports and the composed confidence of colonial administrators, and remained largely unaware of the growing momentum toward independence. When it finally came, it arrived with a speed and force that took many by surprise, as the empire's grip had been weakening long before they knew to look for the cracks.

But there were women, albeit few in number, who sympathized with African nationalist causes and supported peaceful transition efforts. And then there were some who actively opposed independence and became politically involved in defending settler interests. Their mothers were neither.

They had pitched camp on Greg's family estate. Pappi was listening intently to the stories her friends shared, realising that they were the only Kenyan identity she knew. She shivered, feigning a cool breeze blowing her way, and stood up.

'I'll fetch a cardigan,' she said, walking to the tent she was sharing with the girls. She felt alone. She was sitting on the floor of the tent, a cry building up, when Chris appeared at the entrance.

'Are you ok?' Even in the dark, she could tell he knew she was on the verge of tears. She shook her head, which he seemed to see in the dark. He stepped in, squatted beside her.

'Hey, we're all one team, Paps.'

'We're not.' She cried. 'I'm on a team on my own. I don't have a history, or a future.'

'That's not true.'

Chris put his arm around her, her course afro on his face. It had a sweet fragrance which reminded him of the flower garden outside his window. He'd never held anyone that close, and the feeling of not wanting to let her go was overwhelming. She sobbed quietly, aware that his dirty shirt was now also wet with her tears. He'd have to find a way to explain himself to the others.

But when they came out of the tent and reappeared to the group, no one asked anything. They watched them walk back to the campfire, observing them carefully, quietly. But no one asked anything.

Chapter 18

Unexpected Reunion

The Summer Symposium in Uppsala had drawn researchers and academics from around the world. A great number of people walked briskly towards the Nordic Africa Institute where the symposium on *The Future of Africa* was being held. Tony Whitestone was one of them, hurrying to get a seat in the auditorium. He would be presenting some of his work the following day. He smiled at a Swedish woman as he held the door open for her.

He looked around at the filling auditorium, nodded his head to a few of his colleagues. He could not make out what Rolf was saying, amidst all the noise so he smiled and shook his head, mouthing: 'Can't hear you', and Rolf laughed, waving. Tony stumbled over someone's bag and as he bent down to move it aside, his gaze fell on a woman who glowed with familiarity. Her name came to him like a distant echo from the past. *Sue.* He hurriedly apologised to the bag owner, who was engaged in a conversation with the person behind him, and walked on awkwardly in a surprised state. He looked around to make sure, and just caught sight of her craning her neck, trying to find an empty seat, before people blocked his view and he could not see her any longer.

They ran into each other in the lobby two hours later. Tony was following the queue in the cafe, while looking around to see if he could find the familiar face again. Then as he took a step forward, following the slowly moving queue, a woman stood there smiling up at him.

He stared down into her face, 'Sue!'

She laughed radiantly, 'You remembered me! It's wonderful to see you, Tony!' The symposium faded into the background as Tony and Sue embraced. It had been decades since they had last seen each other, their lives having taken them in different directions across the globe.

Tony was laughing along with her. 'How is it possible that you are here?' He asked, wearing a baffled but joyful expression.

'I'd ask you the same question. I didn't know that you lived in Sweden.'

'It's my first time here - Oh no I don't live in Sweden.'

It was becoming impossible to hear each other now. He pulled her away and a few minutes later, they walked out into the July sun, talking at the same time, and trying to listen to each other. Sue lived in Los Angeles. She was a high school geography and history teacher.

Sue's life had been a whirlwind of adventure. She had lived in Scotland, London and now in Los Angeles. 'Tell me about you, Tony.' Sue asked with genuine interest. As Tony began telling her about his wife and children, she listened with the attentiveness of an interested child, laughing when he told a story about a certain Mr. Bird, a relative of Jessica, his wife.

They met many times during the rest of the symposium, reminiscing about the old days, growing up in the Rift Valley. They spoke about Chris, Pappi, Mary-Anne, Roger, Greg and others who were part of their lives. On the last day of the symposium, she said, 'tell me everything about South Africa. Why did you decide to stay?' Tony sighed contentedly, gratified by her company and an incredibly successful symposium.

'It is many years ago, and I cannot quite remember how things had felt like when my family had moved from the Rift Valley to Pretoria.' But he told her the main reason why he had decided to stay, 'I fell in love. Jessica changed my heart and made me want to stay.'

They sat in a restaurant where they had lunch before he drove the rented car back to the airport. Tony was seeing for the first time since he met her that there was sadness in her eyes. Soon they'd both be leaving, and they did not know if or when they would see each other again. She sat in silence, fiddling with her coffee cup. Finally, she looked up at him and said, 'I disowned everyone. Marrying Bradford took me away from all of you.' She broke down.

It was a quiet day, and there were only a few people in the restaurant. *It feels strange,* Tony thought. *Like the whole town has been to the symposium, and now everyone has packed up and left for wherever they came from.*

It had been no secret in 1962 that Sue's family faced serious financial difficulties. Their family estate was burdened with debts at the worst time in history. Tony leaned across the table and put a hand on her arm.

'I heard what happened.' He said carefully. Bradford died in a car accident two years after their wedding.

'I wanted desperately to reach out to one of you,' Sue said, composing herself.

'Why didn't you?'

'I don't know.' She wanted a cigarette. She'd stopped smoking a few years before and had hardly thought of a cigarette until now. Tony was looking at her face, her pain hidden behind her elegant facade. She'd been a year or two older than everyone, and with her beauty, she had everyone paying attention to the smallest details of her life.

'Pappi asked about you many times. She seemed to have been searching for you.'

'I wanted to keep in touch, Tony, but life took us in very different directions.'

Tony nodded. 'You had a rough road.' He said, 'Did you manage to move on?'

'I went back to school. The most healing experience.' She laughed, a genuine and beautiful laughter that brought a smile back to Tony's face.

'You are a courageous woman,' Tony admired her resilience.

'I should reach out to the girls.'

Tony ventured further, 'And perhaps to Greg, Chris, and maybe Roger?'

Sue's smile hinted at mischief as she leaned closer, 'I had moved to New Zealand in the '80s. Roger found me a job as a secretary at a publishing house.'

Tony sat back, a grin beginning to creep across his face, surprised that Roger had never mentioned that chapter of his life.

Chapter 19

Stepping Aside

Pappi sat by the window in the living room working and occasionally looking out of the window. It was August, and late summer filled the air. She could see the neighbours' children running up the little hill just beyond their backyard.

She was shaken off her thoughts by a screeching Judith. The child came rushing into the room with all the energy of a seven year old, and rolled on the sofa. Her older sister followed, with the annoyed anger of a big sister, and the two ran round and round the sofa, shouting this and that and one trying to catch the other in vain. Finally the younger one tore off through the open door and down the stairs. The older one followed suit.

Pappi watched them, smiling at first, then with her mouth agape, trying to say something to stop the fight but not quite saying anything. As the two children ran out of the room, she caught herself laughing. She turned back to her work. Then from the corner of her eye, she caught sight of Jason's Peugeot as it rolled into the parking lot and came to a stop.

Jason opened the front door and the girls rushed to him in great noise. Judith was trying to say something that could not be understood from where Pappi was upstairs. Kate's voice rang out tones higher and clearer than her sister's. Pappi sat there in suspended thoughts, as she half listened to the goings on downstairs.

'There you are gran!' Pappi was shaken out of her reverie but she eagerly turned, smiling at her grandson.

John was halfway across the room, grinning from ear to ear, saying something about having wondered where on earth gran had disappeared to after tea. Pappi stood up and drew him to her side in a half hug, 'I'm glad you didn't give up on me.'

'I'm gonna miss you grandma.'

Pappi kissed his cheek, and before she could say anything, Elizabeth appeared, her hands full of papers. She was saying, 'we must carefully think of the best option, Ma. Jason thinks it's worth paying the little extra if it's going to save you the trouble of having to wait four hours in Amsterdam for your flight.' She stopped and looked at her mother and son, standing by that window.

She looked at the papers in her hands.

'John, go on down and help dad with dinner.' She motioned with her head to the direction of the kitchen and then she repeated more gently, 'Go on darling and help your dad.'

Elizabeth put the papers on the sofa and walked towards her mother. 'Ma. Can we not talk about this again?'

Pappi held her at an arm's length and smiled gently. 'We have talked about it already, Elizabeth. This is something I need to do.'

She thought again how strange it was, that in her fifties she could feel this exciting surge of adventure.

'It feels as though you're walking out of our lives.'

'Well it's not so.' Pappi reassured her, 'We'll have constant communication. And you know, it is time for me to step aside and allow you and Jason to raise your family.'

Just then the phone rang. They let it ring. Someone would pick it up downstairs.

It would be a big change for both. Although she put up a strong front, Pappi knew that it would be difficult for her to be away from her family.

Chapter 20

Tony

Tony folded the letter. 'Yes I'm coming down!' he shouted back to Jessica's third dinner announcement. He grabbed the envelope and put the letter in it as he left the room. Albert's room was across from theirs, and the door was open. A pile of clothes lay on the floor and Albert on his bed, a book in his hands and music playing loudly.

Tony stood at his door and shouted, 'let's go down!'

Albert shouted back 'I'll be there in a minute!'

Albert was the youngest of their children. When they had decided to get married, Jessica had only been eighteen and on her way to medical school. She had grown up in a family of six children and had almost been raised in the Children's Home that her parents ran.

On their second date she had told Tony, 'I won't have any kids.' Tony had immediately thought that she had a medical condition and could not conceive so he had kindly said 'There are countless women that can't have children, Jessica. Don't worry about it.' Before he could assure her that they could always adopt a child from her parent's Children's Home, she laughed and said, 'I wouldn't worry about not being able to have kids. Look at my mom and her six-some - am sure I am as fertile as they come.' Then she took Tony's hand and said, 'I just don't want to have kids.' She had been eighteen then, and three years later, still a medical student, had given birth to Julie, followed seven years later by Rachel. And nine years later Albert came along.

After dinner, Tony reached for the envelope and gave it to Jessica. 'You were right, it was Pappi.' When she had read it, she came over to the couch where Tony sat and said, 'You know, I always expected it.' She smiled. 'Pappi is right in going back. I think it took her much longer than it should have but I am happy she is going back home.'

Home. Tony was looking at Jessica and thinking how much like Pappi she was. The two women had met a few times over the years and since their first acquaintance they had hit it off like old friends. They both had a commitment to people that few people seemed to understand. But *Africa, home for a middle-aged English lawyer?* Tony wondered.

'Tony?'

Jessica was sitting on the coffee table in front of him. 'Where are you honey?'

'Right here.'

'No, you were not.' she laughed. 'You had one of those looks you wear when you're miles away.'

'I did?' Jessica hit him playfully, 'Tell me what you were thinking about.'

And one thing more they had in common, Tony decided, *they never gave up.* Jessica had a persistent way of getting information out of people. Their children never got away with anything if their mother was confronting them. *Actually,* Tony settled with a smile, as he pulled Jessica off the coffee table. *In many ways, my wife is like a lawyer.*

At the end of September Rachel graduated from the University. Relatives and friends would be gathering to celebrate straight after the ceremony at the university.

'She's going to make a great designer.' Jessica said proudly. When Rachel was fourteen years old, she had sewn her own dress for her primary school graduation, and a year later she had surprised everyone by handing each a hand-made gift at Christmas.

'It's a competitive career.' Tony said. He knew little about designing clothes, but that you had to have something different from everyone else to make it. 'It's not that Rachel is not exceptionally good.' He said thoughtfully.

'Well?' Jessica jolted.

'I'm getting old.' Tony mumbled.

She smiled. 'That wasn't it.'

Tony shrugged. 'I am her father, and I want her to be the best there is.'

'But you're not sure she is?'

'It's not that. She will make it big. I just don't want her to struggle to make it.' Then he took the small of her shoulders in his hands, 'Let's celebrate our daughter.'

'Yes.' She smiled up at him.

Julie walked towards them, her young children tagging along.

'Julie, love!' Tony picked up little Jack, who had turned three in August, 'And how are you, Jack?'

Julie had moved with her husband to Namibia two years before. It was a huge separation from everyone, and Jessica liked to cry each time she saw their grandchildren.

'Julie darling. Any signs of a move back home?' She began. It was difficult not seeing the little ones as often as they used to. As the women stood in embrace Tony took the children's hands and walked in search of Rachel.

'Anthony!'

Mr. Bird was Jessica's uncle, whose first name he disliked and insisted on being called Mr. Bird or Uncle Bird.

'Mr. Bird.' Tony answered in greeting.

Mr. Bird clasped Tony's shoulder, supporting himself and breathing heavily.

'I said to myself, Anthony, I said I must speak to you alone before the end of the day.'

Tony waited for him to catch his breath before he reminded him, 'You do know that my name is Tony, Mr. Bird. Anthony is not my name.'

'Anthony is an Englishman's name. And you son - ' He pointed at Tony.

'You're an Englishman, that's who you are.' Mr. Bird finished, straightening himself up. Tony laughed despite himself. Mr. Bird was almost eighty years old and had never lived in England. He however prided himself for having true English roots and must remain Mr. Bird until his death.

'Now, the matter I had in mind,' he continued. 'Regards young Albert.'

Albert was an artist at heart and had loved music since an early age.

'I see the boy's talent is being flawed, so to speak, by this -' He waved his hands wildly, 'today's music variety.' He finished with great displeasure. Anne and Jack were losing patience. Tony picked both up, much to their enjoyment. They looked around gleefully.

'Albert is young.' Tony assured the older man. 'He will find the thing that is just right for him as he grows older.'

'No, no.' Mr. Bird's hand looked for Tony's shoulder again, then seeing as the children were leaning on both, he dropped it rather loudly on his thigh.

With a scowl he said, 'You do not understand, I'm afraid, Anthony. The boy has a talent, and the family must pave his way accordingly.'

Paving Albert's way accordingly included schooling him in a music school in England and separating him from everything that was familiar to him. This was not the first time that Jessica's uncle was bringing this up, and Tony knew it would not be the last.

'I understand Mr. Bird.'

'As I said, my sister Marjorie who lives in England is of the same mind that Albert ought to be sent to a remarkable school that supports talents of such calibre, and she will of course take charge of him.'

Anne and Jack saw their father and squealed in delight. Tony put them down, and they ran to him. He turned to Mr. Bird, 'Really Mr. Bird, that is very much appreciated, but we cannot possibly consider it.'

To turn Albert over to a great-aunt that he had never met was unthinkable. *Plus*, Tony comforted himself, *Jessica would never hear of it*.

He walked back to where Jessica now sat with Albert.

'Don't worry about what he said to you, Tony.' Jessica whispered. Tony put his arm around her. That evening at the small family party back in their home Albert entertained everyone, playing Franz Liszt's, *La Campanella* and later he sang with Rachel.

Chapter 21

Greg

A young woman in a long blue dress walked about the church-yard, glancing at her watch every now and then and looking at the church gate anxiously. Her father had said he would be there ten minutes ago, and now she could not even reach him on his mobile phone.

'Candy,' Jonathan called. She turned round to her becoming brother-in-law. 'Everyone is asking about your dad. Have you reached him?'

Just then, her father pulled up in the family's Holden Commodore, and she hastily rushed to him.

'Daddy! You said you would be here ages ago!'

Greg got out of the car, full of apologies, trying to look beyond his sixteen-year-old daughter in search of her older sister whose wedding it was. Now Candy pulled him away, describing his duties again to him, and reminding him not to confuse her sister with herself. She also reminded him, 'Mom is here. Naturally. Be civil to each other,' adding an emphatic '*Please.*'

'Of course.' He assured her.

'Whatever happened to your car?' Candy asked, and then, 'Does mom know you're borrowing her car?'

'Borrowing!' He started, then looking at his daughter's upturned face he said, 'Of course, my love. I left a message in her answering machine.'

Greg Anderson had a larger-than-life personality. As the founder of Anderson Advertising, he was respected in two distinct circles: those who admired his professional prowess and his daughters.

The transition to societies outside his homeland Kenya had been the hardest for Greg. Life in the bustling cities of the world was a stark contrast, and Greg had struggled to find his footing. His late-night conversations with Tony often revolved around Greg's bankruptcies, rebounds and great business ideas. His spirited quality endeared him to many but also got him into trouble.

He'd been married three times. His first marriage, at twenty-one, had been to an English girl. The union had lasted almost three years before it crumbled under the weight of restlessness and unfulfilled dreams. His second wife had entered his life unexpectedly during a family holiday in Paris. They had impulsively eloped to South Africa, only for the marriage to disintegrate within a few months. Afterward, Greg found himself drifting from one job to another, and for a time he lived with Tony in Pretoria. But Tony's tough-love approach had eventually kicked Greg out, a move intended to help him take control of his life.

With all his savings, Greg had purchased a ticket to Australia, embarking on a journey in search of a fresh start. It was here, in 1978, that he met Linda, the woman who would become his anchor and the mother of his four children. Linda was a music teacher and had adorned their home with a plethora of musical instruments and books. Despite their differences, Greg had fallen deeply in love with her, and their home had become a sanctuary for him. Linda had provided their children the stability Greg sometimes struggled to provide.

She left him just over a year ago because he refused to change.

'What was I to change to?' he muttered under his breath.

'Dad, please. Not now. Now you have got to be *nice,* not just to mom. To everyone.' Candy commanded, shoving her hand through his arm. She said, 'There's aunt Marie,' then quietly she snarled, 'Be nice to her, dad.'

Greg thought he was always nice. He was not prone to anger of any kind, and if anything he went out of his way to make everyone feel good about themselves. Linda's mother loved him, thought he was the kindest of men. Her father, on the other hand, called him a liar. He had said once, *'the only good thing about you Greg, is that you are a good liar. That's why you're so successful at what you do.'* That was shortly before Linda left.

After they had walked in and out of several relatives and friends, they came to the reception area where he was to be civilised and made to recite every word he would say and everything he would do, for the sake of the video recording. Dorothy's wedding was the first in their family and it was to be done properly.

Greg was never one for elaborate formalities or extravagant ceremonies. His down-to-earth nature and knack for simplifying complex matters were qualities that his employees loved about him. This was all Linda's dream idea. He knew Dorothy would not care if no one but herself and her fiancé Jonathan were present at their wedding. Now he smiled around like someone who was thoroughly enjoying himself.

He looked at Candy, 'You look all grown up sweetheart.' He shook his head, 'What happened to my little girls?'
'I'm still here,' She said, her words carrying a reassuring warmth.

Greg saw Linda just before the ceremony began. She stood there talking with friends and relatives, not far away from him, and he stole a glance every now and then. He had been away a lot, and she had been at home too much. He wondered again what he was supposed to change into. *A man of my age, blended with my business as I am - what would become of me?*

The last time he had seen her had been at her brother's funeral months before, and then she had refused to talk to him.

'You look beautiful.' He said to her when they finally could not avoid each other. *She looks more than beautiful*, he thought to himself. Pampered as she was by all her relatives, and her sons, and Candy. Linda was like that. She won everyone's sympathies and affections.

She looked him over. 'You do too. Very nice.' She pointed at his suit, nodding with approval. Her approval meant everything to him and he languished in that as long as it lasted.

'Ready with your lines?' She asked.

He bolted upright and put his fingers in his small pocket, searching for his lines which Candy had scribbled down for him.

'I am ma'am.' He came out with a piece of pink paper.

'Pink?' Linda exclaimed.

He stared at it as though he saw it for the first time. 'Pink.' He said, looking around hastily for his youngest daughter who was responsible for this.

'Greg, pink will not do. Dorothy made it clear she wanted nothing pink!' Linda stated firmly, then looking at his confused expression she took him by the hand to the back of the room where there was a desk and a guest book on it. People were quickly filling the room now, taking their seats. The ceremony would begin in a few minutes. She leafed through the guest book as though she knew what she was looking for and sure enough, there was a piece of blue paper lying between the pages. She quickly snatched it, and scribbled the lines that were on the pink paper. Before Greg could think, they were walking back, a piece of blue paper with his lines on it rested in the small of his pocket.

He sat down next to her, turned to steal a look into her face, could not help smiling. She looked up at him, her clean face the picture of her daughters, a touch of vulnerability crowding her eyes. He quickly bent down and kissed her. Dorothy had said she did not want to be walked down the aisle, because she wanted all attention to herself. They all stood up as she entered, dazzling like a picture.

The wedding was followed by a glamorous reception on the lush grounds of Linda's uncle's holiday house in Country Valley. Greg now listened to his nineteen year old son, Brian, as he told him about his new job at the studio where he was studying. Brian and himself were in many ways like night and day. The only thing they had in common was their ability to convince. Greg had been disappointed when all his attempts to direct Brian into business were unreciprocated. But secretly he was proud of him, for sticking to what he liked.

Keith, his senior, was quiet and reflective. He worked in the marketing department of his father's company.

'Finally someone tied the knot.' Keith said.

'If anyone should be tying knots, it's you.' Greg pointed a finger at Keith as he went on in search of Dorothy. He pretended not to hear when Keith said, 'And you. To mom.'

The truth is, he thought to himself, *I tied that knot 22 years ago, and as far as I am concerned, it is still tied.*

He stole Dorothy away from her doting Jonathan, just before they disappeared to their honeymoon. They strolled hand in hand, like good friends. Dorothy was like him. Careless, unpredictable, and often misunderstood. But she was a strong young woman, and when she found something she liked to do, she did it with all her heart. The problem was that usually she did not find anything she liked to do.

Greg smiled as he listened to her now, talking about the tiny apartment they would move into and the stray cat they had adopted. She'd stay home the first year, she said, taming their stray cat. Everyday joys mattered to Dorothy. *She will do fine,* Greg decided. At twenty, he had been just as näive.

Chapter 22

Rekindling Bonds

It was a week after Dorothy's wedding, and Greg's mind was on Linda. He couldn't wait to see her at Christmas. The telephone rang as he was leaving his office. He went and sank back into his chair.

'Hello? Hello mate!' It was Tony. As always Tony began by briefing Greg on SA sports, particularly football which they had both played at college. They spoke about Dorothy's wedding, and about Linda.

Tony said, 'Well man! You must find a way to bring her along with you next time you are in SA.'

Then Tony had gone on to tell about Pappi's letter concerning her plans to move back to Kenya.

'To live?'

'Yes.'

'Tony, man. At our age? She needs to talk to Roger. She doesn't need to move back.'

'It's home. It's never too late to go back home.' On the other side of the line Tony felt the reality of the event, and quietly with a voice full of emotion, he said, 'Hey, do you remember the New Year party in '75 in London? We made a promise. We said when the youngest of us turned 55-'

'We'd gather at the barn and party.' Greg finished.

There was a tight short laugh at both ends.

'She's turned 55.'

'We were young, Tony. Babes. Roger and Sue should have been there, on account of wisdom and all that. What does Pappi want to move back for?'

Tony sighed. 'Its home, man'

'*Was home.* It was home for all of us many years ago. What do we know about living there now? Besides, isn't Kenya under dictatorial leadership?'

Tony laughed. 'If you've been watching the news, it's soon getting out of it. Days now and they'll have a new president.'

'That's what they promise you in Africa, Tony, but delivery takes decades and meanwhile people die for lack of hope.'

'This time it's the real deal. I can feel it. Pappi can feel it.'

'What about her great life in England?'

'Elizabeth is a big girl,' Tony laughed. 'And the firm - they're way too busy in London to notice she's gone.'

'I still think she should talk to Roger. He has been travelling back and forth between Africa and New Zealand long enough. He'll understand what Pappi is putting herself through.'

Tony said quietly, 'Greg, bottom line is, Pappi needs our support. She's moving there. And has a big project on her shoulders. She will need all the support we can give her.'

Greg was looking at an old picture of Linda and the children that stood at his desk. Above it on the wall hung an even older picture. In it were Tony, Chris, Pappi, MaryAnne, Sue, Roger and himself. It was taken at the New Year's party in 1963, outside Pappi's barn. The memories of that night flooded back. Their excitement as they all worked together to decorate the barn and prepare for the upcoming party. He and Mary-Anne held hands in the picture. Sue leaned on Roger's shoulder. Yet, it was the unspoken sentiments between Chris and Pappi that had everyone waiting in anticipation.

'And Chris?' Greg asked.

'Chris is in. You know he's in.'

'Anything for Paps. Perhaps this will be the time he finally faces the truth?'

Tony chuckled. 'I think now's the time.'

He smiled. 'Ok Tony. I'm in.'

Chapter 23

The verge of Change

Jason got home just as Elizabeth came up with the news at eight. Pappi hushed him silent. She had been waiting for an update of the latest news on Kenyan politics. There was not much that she did not already know, but it always seemed more real to her to see moving pictures and hear the voice of the broadcaster. It was December 2002, and all signs pointed to Mwai Kibaki becoming Kenya's next president, bringing an end to KANU's long reign after President Moi. Few still believed that the late President Kenyatta's son, Uhuru Kenyatta, would win. *But what do I know of this?* Pappi muttered. She was after-all, a spectator, as she had been all her life.

Mary-Anne had commented at one time, 'So what if you were just a spectator? Weren't we all?'

To which she had replied, 'Like our mothers.'

'All our mothers. And they were grown-ups. You think they cared for any politics? They did not care if London ruled - as long as they were let to live in their nice houses.'

Pappi laughed, happy to distract herself.

In all their reminisces Mary-Anne never remembered that *they* were white, and *she* was black. Pappi had a unique identity struggle. In her teens she developed a disconnection from her parents, and began to feel isolation. She remembered at 14, when her parents had sat her down for the first serious conversation about coming of age. The atmosphere in the room had reflected their stern expressions.

Her mother began, 'Pappi, you're now a young lady. It's inappropriate for a young lady to play with boys in the same way you did as a child.'

Her father picked up immediately, 'Your friendship with Chris, is there something we need to know?'

'Father!' Pappi exclaimed. She did not understand what was concerning about a boy she'd known all her life. 'Chris is like a brother to me. You know that!'

'It didn't seem that way two days ago!' Her mother snapped, shooing the servant who brought tea away.

A week ago, Pappi remembered. She'd fallen and sprained her ankle during their hike up a hill. Chris and Tony had helped her down to the car and Chris had scooped her out of his father's pickup when they dropped her home. Pappi felt her heart sink. It did not surprise her that close friendships with the opposite sex were discouraged in her home. But being told to distance herself from Chris was something she hadn't expected.

As time passed and Pappi turned 15, her parents sat her down for another talk. Her mother started, 'Pappi, we've thought about this, and we feel that it would be appropriate for you to consider a relationship with a young man from our church, someone who shares your origin.'

Her father added, 'It is essential that you marry someone who understands you.'

Pappi felt a whirlwind of emotions - confusion, frustration, a sense of being trapped between her parents' expectations and her own. She felt the need to assert her independence and find her own path. No one understood her as Chris did. It was 1962 and many of their neighbours were leaving the country. She knew it was a matter of time before her friends' families packed them up and left. A sense of loneliness began to creep in.

'A few days, and all this will be over,' Jason was saying. He looked over at Pappi, who nodded. Her eyes were glued on the TV screen, but she was deep in thought. Jason left the room, stopping at the study to say hello to the girls, who were both at the computer. He could hear John drumming softly in his room. Once Elizabeth was home, the house would be full of life again.

Pappi walked over to the phone and dialled Mary-Anne's number.

'It's me May.'

'How are you?' Mary-Anne shouted.

'Tired.'

'You're thinking far too much about Kenya.'

'What else is there to think?'

'Roger's and Sue's visit for Christmas, for starters. We have a lot to prepare. Besides, you don't want fatigue to disqualify you from the work you have in mind.' Mary-Anne said firmly.

'I know, and I'm not worrying.' Pappi repeated this to herself, *I am not worrying.*

'Whatever will happen out of those elections will take the country one step forward. And it shall not affect my decision to move back.'

'How's the house coming along?'

Pappi had begun renovations of the old farmhouse where she grew up earlier in the summer. Timotheo had found a company that would do all the work, from plumbing to painting.

'Good. It's going really well. Timotheo sends me pictures as often as he'll visit the site. Did you know they're doing landscaping too?'

'Jack of all trades?' Mary-Anne laughed.

'Yep, and they asked about the barn.'

'What about the barn?' Mary-Anne asked sharply.

'You know, what to do about it. It's run-down and all.'

'You don't let them touch that barn Paps. That's our part. We'll restore the barn.' Mary-Anne said firmly.

The barn held most of their memories growing up. It was the gathering place for all seven of them. It was the place where sleepovers were done in their younger years when the boys were allowed to sleep over, and later when they could sneak out. It was a place of secrets, promises and first kisses. A sacred place. In all the years the property had been rented out, the barn had remained strictly off limits. It did not contain much that was valuable. But the junk inside was invaluable.

Later that night as she lay on her bed, Pappi remembered the night before she and Elizabeth left Kenya. She had been curled on the floor of her bedroom sorting Elizabeth's clothes and trying to guess the weight of the two luggages already packed. When finally she got into bed, she was surprised to find Elizabeth in there, wide awake.

'Lizzie! What are you doing here? Haven't you been asleep in your bed?'

'Yes I have.' She lied.

'I was packing your clothes.'

'OK.'

'You can sleep here with me if you want.'

'OK. Goodnight mommy.'

'Good night Lizzie.'

Chapter 24

Roger

There was a charged sense of anticipation and change in every conversation across Kenya. President Daniel Toroitich Arap Moi had held the reins of power for 24 years, and his imminent departure was the topic of fervent discussion.

In the noisy marketplaces where traders gathered to sell their wares, opinions about Moi's tenure were mostly unified. Very few expressed gratitude for the relative stability during the start of his rule. President Moi's philosophy of *'Nyayo'* called for Kenyans to follow the footsteps of national unity and peaceful development, which arguably worked to one's benefit as long as things remained as they were. No opposing opinions were welcome. Yet although Kenya had remained a poor country, it had a number of successes including becoming a multiparty democracy and the economy remaining above that of the rest of Eastern African countries.

Now most of the younger generation yearned for a fresh start and a break from what they perceived as stagnation, and failure to embrace and make the most of the country's resources and the rich tribal cultures in the country. Businesses, both large and small, demanded change. Entrepreneurs that had weathered economic fluctuations throughout Moi's presidency looked forward to new opportunities. The prospect of a more open and dynamic economic framework fueled their optimism.

Jubilant students had left their high schools at the end of November after their Kenya Certificate of Secondary Education examination, proudly aware of the fact that they would be entering an historical era the following year. In the universities political discourse was impassioned. Many were eager for an era marked by greater transparency, accountability, and social progress. Campaign posters adorned lampposts and political rallies drew throngs of supporters of a new regime.

Roger finished his lunch and picked up his tray. It was Monday the sixteenth of December and he was giving his last lecture for the year. Two days and he would be flying to England to meet Sue. They'd be having Christmas with Pappi, Chris, Mary-Anne and Patrick. He walked to the lecture room thinking of Pappi's letter about her move back to Kenya. He had said matter of factly when they spoke on the phone, 'Why not? You'll find more fun things to do here than you'll ever find in all of Europe.' As he neared the auditorium, he remembered the year of Kenyan independence.

It was February 1963, and Derek Church was driving to Nairobi to deliver his speech. His sons were with him. Dean, twenty-three, Nathan, twenty-one, and Roger, nineteen. Nairobi was crowded with people, banners flew everywhere, and finding a place to park the car was almost impossible. Roger remembered that particular day because it stirred in him an awareness of not belonging, and for the first time, he glimpsed a kind of freedom he hadn't realised was missing. He understood what was happening in the country, *but there's something that changes you when you see it for yourself*, he thought. When the headlines become faces and the stories come alive.

It was also this period of the year that Sue yielded to the weight of her family's financial collapse, agreeing to bail them out by marrying Bradford. For many settlers, the exit routes were swiftly narrowing. Some packed their belongings with brittle resignation, others scrambled to fasten themselves to what power remained. For Sue's family, the Bradfords were the remaining lifeline. No one else could buy their property. The Bradford's entanglement with the emergent political order ensured their place in Kenya's postcolonial future. And so for a fraction of the value of the property, they helped Sue's family to start a new life in England.

David Bradford was best known as Bradford, as though his given name had slipped away at childhood. He was an only child, an heir to more than property - he would inherit the family's alliances. But everyone knew that David had no taste for the predictable rhythms of power. It was widely presumed that he would never marry. The women introduced to him at formal dinner parties often left with polite stories of a man pleasant enough, but distant, as though his attentions were turned to something just beyond the visible horizon. His mother, a woman deeply attuned to the power of her station, had once despaired in private, confessing to a friend over tea that her boy 'has mistaken life for literature.' And so, when the arrangement with Sue's family was sealed, it was in astonishment - that there would be a union at all - that people whispered.

But David's parents knew that their son was ill-fitted for Kenya, uninterested in managing estates, and altogether indifferent to allegiances that propped up families like theirs. Under the emerging Kenyan regime, his chances of survival were even slighter. They wanted a life in England for him, where his sensitivities might be a virtue rather than a liability. And Sue, though she may not have known it at first, was his passage out.

Roger began his lecture.

'A man in his late fifties stops suddenly at the traffic jam in Jogoo Road,' He paced the floor slowly, 'he is well aware that it may be another ten minutes before he has to start the engine again. On the lane next to him, a slightly older man halts. A second later they recognised each other.

'Hey *Bwana*! *Namna gani*?' One says to the other.

'Besides the hustles of getting ready for a new government, we're very well!' The other replies. They laugh, knowing without explanations that they both shared in the hustles of getting ready for a new government.

The students laughed, moving slightly in their seats, relieved and expectant. The men in Roger's tale could have been their fathers and brothers. Roger understood their excitement and knew well how much hope they had for a new government.

'Kenya has gone through a series of stages in the last forty years.' He continued. He taught an intensive course once a year in the university of Nairobi. The auditorium was full, which was strange, given that it was a week before Christmas.

'Colonial administration had driven the nation to a state of social and political anxiety - a pressing urgency for systemic change. The country had transitioned from its historically decentralized, tribe-based governance structures to an externally imposed colonial system that disrupted indigenous autonomy. You would expect that because all Kenya had endured the same struggle and shared the deep feelings of wanting to own what belonged to them, they had become more unified in their thinking and initiatives.'

He paused here. Someone coughed. Several moved forward in their seats. Someone raised their hand and Roger nodded.

'It's possible that many of us are still tribal in our thinking.' A student said.

'We have a bigger battle to overcome before we can be fully unified.' Another student added.

Several hands were up. Roger nodded to a student in the front seat.

'We are more unified now than we were before independence -'

'I disagree.' Roger turned and nodded to a young man in the back row. 'Before independence we followed rules we did not like. After independence how well we managed to be a democratic republic has come out in the last twenty four years. Not very well, sir.' Students laughed.

Roger continued, 'Once the difficult journey to independence was over began the long and complicated journey of building and managing the nation. The government, society, infrastructure, international relationships.' Roger continued pacing up and down the floor. 'Education became more widespread. During colonial rule, the line between education and politics was narrow. There was a tendency toward education for social and political control.' He had his finger on his lips, flashing back to the meeting he had attended with his brothers and father in 1963.

'By the native Kenyan?' A girl asked. Before Roger could answer the small boy from the back row made to stand up again as he answered her. 'They needed competence to overrule.'

In the meeting were four Kenyan men, each with academic achievements higher than his father's, but to whose disadvantage the meeting had ended.

'Yes. Education was a key for them to gain competence and also a weapon to protect what was theirs. After independence more adults enrolled in adult educational institutions and although there was prejudice against educating girls, many children and youth were put to schools. However there was also a great need for training personnel to fill high level positions that had just been recently vacated by the colonial authority. This was especially important if the country was to maintain the level of development into which the nation had arrived.'

It was the longest day of the week for Roger. This evening he would be having dinner with several colleagues. He knew what most of the conversation would be about. The ruling party, KANU, and the president, were a household name. Now both stood on the peak of a volcanic mountain. Any minute and the mountain would erupt.

Chapter 25

A Walk in Kingston Gate

Mary-Anne and Pappi strolled leisurely along a winding path in Kingston Gate. Mary-Anne's energetic huskies weaved in and out of the sidewalk with an unquenchable exuberance. People bustled past them, from work or to nearby cafes and restaurants. It had become somewhat of a tradition for the two to meet up for a walk and to share a meal at one of their favourite restaurants. Either in Kensington or Richmond. Today Mary-Anne took a taxi to Richmond.

'You're heading back to Kenya soon!' She exclaimed, her blue eyes sparkling with envy as they walked side by side.

'Yes, flying out in a few weeks, still can't believe it.' And then, 'And you May - taking a taxi to Richmond! I know you have more money than many of us put together, but it's even faster to take the tube!'

The very first event she'll hold in Kenya would be to collect money that would help to establish larger development work with women and children. She was keen on saving every dime. Mary-Anne had never been short of anything, and was overwhelmingly generous in funding Pappi's bazaar.

'It wasn't much, honest. It's just my ankle being what it is,' she pretended to limp, 'I couldn't walk the two kilometres to the subway station.'

'It's hardly a kilometre,' grumbled Pappi. They stopped at the zebra crossing.

'And with the dogs.'

'The dogs love the tube.' Pappi rolled her eyes, her ebony skin gleaming in the winter sunlight. '*Foundations for Change*,' She wrote in the air, grinning in satisfaction. 'Isn't that catchy?'

'Of course, thanks to me. It was all my idea, but I'm happy to share.' Mary-Anne said. They stopped outside L'Opossum. 'Should we try something else for a change, what do you think?'

Pappi agreed, and they kept walking. 'I can't wait to see the project kickoff.' She said thoughtfully.

Mary-Anne nodded. She knew how dedicated Pappi was in her work, and her goal to make a tangible difference in the lives of women and children was gaining support from many of their acquaintances. 'Your passion for this cause is inspiring. Between you and I,' Mary-Anne gave her an honest glance as she pulled the door open to Amuse Bouche. The huskies rushed in. 'I've been dreaming of ways I could convince Patrick to let me stay longer in Kenya when I come to the bazaar.'

'I hope he'll be ok with that. You're fortunate to have found someone as considerate as Patrick.'

'And how fortunate *he is*, to have found a great woman like me.'

'Absolutely right.' Pappi agreed, starting to leaf through the menu and then stopping. She looked over at Mary-Anne, 'Is everything ok?'

'Yes, fine.'

'You two have never been apart for more than a weekend. Talk to me.'

'It's nothing, just that all this talk about you leaving, and it being so easy for you to go places. It's never been like that with me, you know.'

Pappi put the menu down and in a reassuring voice said, 'Hey, if it's any consolation, I wish a great guy would try to stop me from leaving.' They held hands across the table, looked at each and laughed. Then with a serious look on her face, Mary-Anne said, 'If you gave Chris a reason to, he'd stop you.'

This was one of the familiar roads they'd been on for decades. Pappi had waited for Chris to take the initiative. She hated that she couldn't articulate even to her closest friend, the boundaries that had been ingrained in her as a teenager, sternly forbidding her from pursuing a relationship with Chris.

''Cos I know you, Paps. It's not the traditional gender roles that you're concerned about. And you've loved this man all your life.'

'It's complicated.' She sighed, 'Now,' She changed the subject, trying to look cheerful. 'I tell you what, since you're keen on dreaming. Why don't you convince Patrick to take time off work, and join you for a lengthy holiday in the Rift Valley, after the bazaar in February?'

Mary-Anne chuckled. 'Well, what a splendid idea! We've been meaning to go on a second honeymoon for some time, and this could be the perfect opportunity. Patrick does love the idea of exploring Kenya with me.'

Pappi's heart warmed as she listened to Mary-Anne beginning to make plans. They'd come a long way and been in so much trouble together over the years. She remembered their well-intentioned predicaments, as when they misguidedly tried to set up Patrick's older sister on a date with a married man. And when they tried to cure Chris's stomach flu with an array of herbal remedies they'd discovered through their late-night google searches. She smiled now, looking through the menu and nodding in agreement as Mary-Anne talked.

Chapter 26

Mary-Anne

Mary-Anne's family home was nestled between two other estates. Her father was frequently away on business trips, leaving her mother ample time to immerse in the social scene of the White Highlands. Their mother wasn't particularly beautiful, but with her tall stature she was a striking figure in the socialite circles of their community.

She dreamed of grooming her girls for a refined and sophisticated life, envisioning a future where Mary-Anne and her sister Fay would be impeccably prepared for high society, possibly in England, should the uprisings in Kenya amount to the country's independence. She had strict notions of propriety and femininity, which contrasted sharply with Mary-Anne's spirited and independent nature.

Mary-Anne's world was made up of her friends, particularly Pappi and their circle of companions. Pappi's vivacious spirit and love for adventure had a way of drawing Mary-Anne into escapades that defied societal expectations. By the time she was a young teenager, her mother's plans of grooming her into a polished young lady were vanishing. She disapproved of Pappi's influence on her daughter, but particularly Mary-Anne's frequent company of boys, Greg in particular.

It was natural that Mary-Anne liked Greg; she was easy to make laugh, and Greg had an infectious humour. He also had an uncanny ability to make people feel comfortable around him.

When at 15 Mary-Anne became a tad heavier than the rest of the girls and her mother made an issue of it, it was to Greg that she turned. Her mother's disapproval was no secret. 'Darling, you're still squirming in mud with this boy. He's clearly without a goal in life!'

'That's not fair, mother. And we're not in England exactly. Things are different here.'

Her mother winced, as though physically wounded. 'Societal norms have no boundaries, young lady! England or the colonies, I want you moulded into a proper lady, groomed for the world of privilege that you were born into!'

It was a week after the new year in 1963, and although she'd just been there for new year celebrations, Mary-Anne was sleeping over at Pappi's house. They had planned to gather at the barn. Pappi's parents were on a retreat near Lake Victoria, and had left Pappi in the care of a trainee missionary, a young woman who slept like a log. When she retired to bed, the girls managed to sneak out into the confines of the barn, where the rest of their group were waiting. A dimly lit lantern hung on the roof, and the old oak table stood in the midst of hay and other animal feeds stacked in sacks. So much had been taking place around the country, and many families had moved to England or elsewhere at the turn of the year. Sue sat next to Roger, her head resting on his shoulder. The flickering lantern cast shadows on the rustic walls, creating a cosy atmosphere. But unlike the new year party and countless other nights in the barn, tonight was forlorn.

Tony's family would be relocating to South Africa. He talked about his impending departure. Mary-Anne, cradled in Greg's arms, contemplated the idea of eloping with Greg, but with no clear destination in mind. Roger, with Sue's hair all over his shoulder, told everyone what they already knew. He and Sue planned to move to England to go to college. They were older than the others.

Pappi's uncertain future loomed over her thoughts, but she avoided thinking of the undefined path ahead of her. The political state in the country added to the complexity of their emotions. They pondered what independence would mean for their generation. An overwhelming sense of change. She sat between Tony and Chris, and now Chris put his arm around her shoulders.

As the night deepened, the group fished out their hidden leftover snacks from the new year's party. Roger and Chris had smuggled bottles of cider. And to everyone's surprise, so had Tony. The girls had brought slices of Victoria sponge cake, cucumber sandwiches with crusts removed, mini sausage rolls, and Sue had even brought her mom's freshly baked scones with clotted cream and jam. Mary-Anne unwrapped the snacks from the previous party - crispy bhajias, salted peanuts and a selection of biscuits and cookies and laid them all on the oak table.

The party continued into the night, bellowing the 1960s hits: *'Stand by Me'* and *'Rock Around The Clock.'* Their faces flushed from the effects of the alcohol. Slowly they settled in among the hay and sacks, the barn now filled with the soft symphony of snores and occasional giggles.

Chapter 27

The Tea

Pappi smiled, watching Elizabeth's reflection in the mirror as she came down the stairs. 'What's so amusing?' Elizabeth asked.

'You look stunning,' She said.

From the kitchen, Jason shouted, 'Tea time!'

'Your Jason is a good man.'

Elizabeth laughed. 'He's the best.'

'That makes me happy.' It more than made her happy. It comforted Pappi to know that her daughter and grandchildren were in good hands. Jason was walking towards them, a kitchen cloth hanging over his shoulder, saying, 'I've been in love with this girl every day since I laid eyes on her.'

The doorbell rang. Pappi was still smiling when she opened it.

Chris' frame filled the doorway. He was a striking height, and had maintained his rugged yet handsome appearance, now more seasoned in his 50s. His dedication to cricket and frequent runs had paid off, keeping him in great shape. He walked in, a warm smile revealing his approachable nature.

'Come in, come in!' Pappi took his hand and drew him in.

'You certainly look happy to see me.'

'Why wouldn't I be?' she shot him a glance.

'Good to see you, Chris!' Jason said, rushing to the living room and returning quickly with a copy of Chris's *Breaking Barriers*. 'You know, you managed to touch on some really crucial issues in this book. If ever there was a time for the redemption of Northern Ireland. Your book is very timely sir!'

'Well, thank you!'

Jason had prepared tea on the porch, a newly added part of the house they'd only just finished furnishing. Though it was December in London, the porch was now glassed in and comfortably heated, making it a cosy retreat even in winter. Chris exclaimed how beautiful it was. 'Isn't it lovely?' Elizabeth added, moving things around on the table as they sat down.

They talked about Chris's new book. *Breaking Barriers* held significant meaning in the context of the history of Northern Ireland and the contemporary political climate. 'There's hardly a country that's not recovering from something,' Elizabeth said. 'Some recoveries are just more special than others. Look at Northern Ireland,' Jason replied, 'Still recovering from decades of sectarian violence,'

The sectarian violence he referred to had divided the Catholic nationalist and Protestant unionist communities. Jason had grown up in a traditionally Protestant Loyalist community of East Belfast. Chris's family roots were hinged in Northern Ireland as well, and he and Jason had shared many conversations about the region in the past years.

As he listened to them talking, Chris turned to Pappi. She sat across from him, her chin resting on one hand, now smiling with him. Her other hand lay on the table, and without thinking, he placed his hand gently over it. The golden rays of the sunset caressed her complexion, creating a radiant glow on her skin. Her hair, a cascade of dark, lustrous curls, framed her forehead. *Like an exquisite work of art,* Chris thought, mesmerised by her beauty. He squeezed her hand, which she quickly withdrew, her dark eyes looking away.

'You will know better than anyone Jason,' Chris composed himself, bouncing back to the conversation at the table, 'that the question is about the complexities of identity, history and political ideologies that have fueled conflict in Northern Ireland.'

'Aye. It's a broad conversation we need to have - on healing and reconciliation. Fragile peace is all we've known in Northern Ireland.' Jason was referring to The Good Friday Agreement that had brought a ceasefire and established The Northern Ireland Assembly, but that had yet to fully complete the reconciliation process.

After tea, Chris followed Pappi up the stairs to the part of the house that was her home. 'How's your mom?' She asked.

'Frail, I'm afraid.'

They settled in Pappi's living room area.

'I'm sorry to hear that. Fordwich had no life to offer your parents. I said that then and I say it now.' Chris's mother was once a robust presence but life in England had worn her thin. The transition from their vibrant life in Kenya to the solitude of Fordwich had taken its toll over the years.

'Well, it had to be their decision. Mom's inheritance would have gone to waste if they hadn't moved there. None of us wanted it. Besides,' Chris added, 'There was no life anywhere in England for them anyway. It didn't really matter where they settled.'

Chris's dad had died a few years earlier, and his eldest sister had moved in to take care of their mother.

'I have my tickets now.' Pappi informed. 'Timotheo and Njoki have invited me to stay at their house during the first weeks. They will not hear otherwise.'

'And just as well. It's not right for you to move to Njoro by yourself.'

Pappi stood up. 'What will you have?'

'Something strong. Rough week at the bank.'

'Brandy?'

'Yes please.'

'Paps,' Chris started, 'Stay with Timotheo, until the rest of us can come. It's not right for you to move to the farm on your own.'

'I will be fine.' She handed him the drink. 'Timotheo has me covered. He's hired a watchman.' She grinned. 'Absolutely unnecessary.'

'Absolutely necessary,' Chris stated. 'He needs to install a digital security system in the house, I'll talk to him about it.' Chris said, with all seriousness.

Pappi smiled. 'Honestly Chris. There's no need.'

She was still standing. He stretched out his hand, which she took and allowed him to pull her gently to the couch next to him. He took Pappi's drink from her hand and put both their drinks on the table in front of them.

'I've something to tell you.' He said. Pappi searched his eyes, and without saying anything, nodded.

'I've asked for leave. I can stay longer in Kenya after the bazaar.'

Pappi knew how demanding Chris's work was, and she felt guilty for imposing on him.

'Chris, you didn't have to do that,' she started, her voice a mix of surprise and gratitude. 'I know how busy you've been, and this really isn't the best time for you to take leave.'

'Being there for you is what matters most to me.' He stated. For a moment, neither of them spoke. The years of friendship and quiet loyalty filled the silence. Then Chris leaned in, closing the gap between them. Pappi had never been more acutely aware of their unspoken connection that had sustained them through the years. Their lips finally met in a hesitant kiss.

'He's here!' John called from downstairs. 'Gran! Roger's here!'

They pulled away, their eyes smiling at each other.

Chapter 28

A Christmas toast

Their reunion filled Pappi's house with nostalgia. The years had done nothing to change how they related to each other. Mary-Anne lifted her glass of champagne. 'A toast to us,' she called jovially.

'To us!' They cheered.

Someone suggested calling Tony and Greg to bring them into the moment. They gathered around Roger's phone, cheering as Greg answered. His bemused voice drifted through the receiver, reminding them it was the middle of the night in Brisbane. Still, he laughed and joined in their celebration. Tony, just as sleepy on his end, joined from another timezone, lifting a glass of milk in a sleepy toast and sending his best wishes.

The Christmas dinner included a succulent roast turkey with all the trimmings, a fragrant biryani that reminded them of Kenya's diverse cuisine, buttery mashed potatoes, and fresh vegetables from the local market. The centrepiece was a rich, homemade fruitcake that Mary-Anne brought. The fireplace created a cosy atmosphere, crackling merrily as they shared stories of their lives and chatted lightheartedly about Pappi's charity bazaar.

'I still can't believe you bottled your love all these years!' Sue exclaimed, watching Chris brush a strand of stray curly hair off Pappi's face.

'We watched him suffer, year after year.' Patrick chimed in with his serious demeanor. They laughed, lifting their glasses and drinking to love.

'I have some good news to share,' Pappi declared at one point in the evening, 'we've got some confirmed high-profile names for the bazaar.'

She shared some of the confirmations she'd already received. 'To be honest,' she began, 'some of these confirmations surprised me, and I have Timotheo to thank for that. We've secured one of the presidential candidates to deliver the keynote address.'

There was a murmur of impressed reactions.

'That's no small achievement,' Patrick said, raising his eyebrows. 'Do you think security will be a concern, with a presidential candidate there?'

'Timotheo is already coordinating with the local authorities and his contacts in Nairobi,' Pappi assured him. 'They're used to handling these things.'

'Besides,' Roger added, 'The elections will be done by then. If our keynote speaker will be the Head of State, I am sure the State will handle the security.'

'We also have senior representatives from the UN attending, and a few regional heads from the World Bank and UNICEF have shown interest. All your contacts have been invaluable. We've also drawn interest from Kenyan and international experts - across education, agriculture, and public health.'

'You're practically organising a summit,' Roger said, lowering his cognac with a soft clink. 'I expected a good turnout, but this is something else.'

'You've done brilliantly, Paps.' Chris put an arm around her shoulders, 'we're all proud of you.'

'Well, I wouldn't have known whom to approach without your networks,' Pappi smiled warmly at the group.

'It's going to be extraordinary.' Sue chimed in, her voice bright. 'With that kind of guest list, the bazaar could raise more than we ever hoped.'

'Exactly,' Mary-Anne agreed, 'and, you've managed to place it on the right people's agendas.'

'You're creating something with real weight, Pappi.' Patrick said. 'I think we've only just started to realise how big this could get.'

There was a moment of shared understanding. Their lives would shift as Pappi returned to Kenya.

Chapter 29

Jomo Kenyatta Airport

It was the fourth of January 2003. Pappi sat glued to the little screen in front of her. Since boarding the Kenya airways from Amsterdam she had felt as though she had arrived. As if all the people in the plane were part of those she would be seeing everyday, for a long time. She had not been able to eat much, but she had drank some orange juice at dinner, and then fallen asleep for an hour. The rest of the time she had sat glued to the small screen in front of her. Now they were ten minutes away from the grounds of the Jomo Kenyatta airport, from where her little Elizabeth and herself had left the country in 1974. Although it was many years ago, she found herself seeing that day in her mind's eyes.

Elizabeth clutched her index finger with her small hand and walked carefully beside her. All goodbyes said, they never looked back. Timotheo and his family stood there watching them go, Njoki's chest heaving with sorrow, their own small children too bewildered to cry. They had been family to Pappi for three years. On the other end, at Heathrow airport, Pappi's parents would be waiting for them. Pappi had spoken on the phone with them that morning during the hassles of last minute packing. Her father had been calm and instructive as always. As they boarded their flight Pappi wondered what life had in store for them in England.

Now they were closing in on the grounds. The pilot's voice could be heard loud and clear, wishing the passengers a good stay and advising those on transit where to go. Pappi wondered briefly about the others who had yet to continue their journey to some other country. Somehow, she found myself wondering - rather foolishly, like a child - if they too had histories to face wherever they were heading.

There was a great commotion at the customs. A huge crowd of tourists and other foreigners formed a long queue, waiting for their visas. After trying to wage her way through, Pappi realised that she no longer possessed a Kenyan passport. She was a visitor in her own country. A little shaken by this memory that she had abandoned for the last eleven hours, she went back to the end of the queue.

People jostled past her. Pappi stood, waiting for a familiar face to come gaily towards her, and also in wonder. The airport looked much smaller than she remembered. She noticed that the guests were not met inside the arrival hall any more. Through the glass window, she could see people holding banners with the names of the guests they were waiting for. Pappi wondered for a second if Timotheo and Njoki would remember what she looked like. She wondered if they had a banner with her name on it. She pulled her luggage and busily laid it on the trolley. She had several, and having retrieved all of them, she straightened her back and turned her trolley around, ready to vacate the comfort of the arrival hall.

PART 3

The Return

2003

Chapter 30

Pappi's Return

Rosina had wondered how prepared Pappi was to return to Kenya. But as she watched her walk, upright and with a swift and sure step, she felt convinced that she was. Her shoulders were bare, revealing the soft skin of her upper arms, emphasising her adorned neck, covered in African jewellery bought years ago at an exhibition in London. Her parents had been concerned that Pappi was firm in her decision to return to live in a country that no longer recognised her as a citizen, and where she had missed on the last thirty years of progress or the decline of it.

After the usual hugs and pleasantries, they began the drive to Ngong Hills, where Pappi would stay with Rosina's parents.

'Dad told me to apologise on their behalf,' Rosina was saying, 'He got caught up at work, and Mum was too nervous to drive to the airport alone. She's waiting at home, really excited to see you.'

'No need to apologise, I completely understand. And how lovely that you came to get me.'

'It's been very hot lately.' Rosina warned.

Pappi had packed everything she knew she would need, and that included everything. 'Ah, the good old heat. How are you all coping with it?'

'We survive - with lots of cold drinks and a fan that never gets turned off.'

'Some things never change,' Pappi chuckled. 'I suppose I'll have to get used to it all over again.'

'Don't worry, we'll ease you back in gently,' Rosina promised, with a laugh. 'Mom has made sure there's a fan everywhere in the house. Just for you.' She finished with a smile.

Pappi thought of Elizabeth, just a few years younger than Rosina, and wondered what she was doing now on her day off.

'What joy. Such joy!' The housekeeper stood at the entrance of Pappi's room, holding a bunch of clean towels and smiling gaily at Pappi. Muthoni must have been somewhere around her late fifties, and had first worked for Timotheo's parents. 'Muthoni, you are so kind. You must tell me all about the events of thirty years while I have been away.' Muthoni laughed heartily, saying that she had been sure Pappi would not remember her, what with all those years. But now that Pappi remembered her, Muthoni promised to tell her everything once she was settled.

It was the second day since her arrival, and there'd been many people coming and going from Timotheo's house, in honour of Pappi's return. She did not know most of the people, but they made her feel instantly welcome, as though she had never left. Dinner had been served twice already today, as the second lot could not keep time and therefore missed the first dinner. Pappi was surprised at the amount of energy her hosts had, entertaining dozens of people every few hours and always keeping conversation going.

When she couldn't take it any more she found solace in her nice bedroom, the one that had been Gilbert's. Now the wall that used to separate Gilbert's and Rosina's rooms no longer existed. Instead a cosy spacious guestroom had emerged. Muthoni had brought in an assortment of things that Pappi would be needing, including a large bowl of mixed nuts. Above the chimney was a framed photo of the family. It was taken in 1970, on professor Muriuki's 50th birthday. She had been there. Pappi had needed them so much after the departure of her friends, and her parents. They'd made her feel at home.

Chapter 31

Nairobi at a Glimpse

Nairobi was not the same town she used to know thirty years back. Although she did not know it thoroughly well even those years, now she found that she could not go anywhere on her own within the city centre. It was over two weeks since she had arrived. Everyone had been wonderful. After days of wrestling with self-doubt and feeling overwhelmed, Pappi sat at breakfast one day with Njoki, and together they began to plan what they'd need for the bazaar. Njoki's support gradually gave Pappi the renewed sense of excitement she had initially had.

Rosina and Pappi were driving along Uhuru highway. Rosina was dressed very smartly in a short black skirt and a nicely fitting black blazer. Underneath the blazer a silk yellow blouse completed her elegant appearance. Pappi wore her all-purpose jeans and a white t-shirt written on the back *Rally for Christ* that she'd bought a week before in the market square in Kiambu. They were going to Nakumatt, one of the biggest in the country along Uhuru highway, and Pappi was as excited as a child. She already missed Safeways, and even the smaller convenient stores all around the blocks in London.

'You'll be surprised at the variety we have in Nakumatt. I'll be very surprised if there's something you cannot find in Nakumatt.'

Rosina swung the car to a parking place and allowed the guard to open the door for her. Pappi hopped off her seat and looked up at the large building which housed the supermarket. Once inside, she realised that Rosina was right. Nakumatt was a bustling, well-organized marketplace under one roof, reflecting the city's rapid growth. She was struck by its scale and modernity. The store was divided into clear sections where shoppers could find everything they needed - from furniture and household goods to stationery and a wide range of food products. Friendly staff moved efficiently among the aisles, ready to assist customers. It was unlike any shopping experience she had known before.

There were shoppers from all over the world. Pappi had intended to search for products she'd normally buy from her corner store back in London. But now she decided to buy Kenyan products, not just to promote the economy but also to get a feel of integration.

When they got the shopping bags into the trunk Rosina said, 'I don't have to be at the office until 1pm. How about you and I take a drive through town a bit and then get something to eat?'

Pappi loved the idea. They first drove through the industrial area, and then, just off Jogoo Road, Pappi asked Rosina to stop. She had caught sight of a small street market. The stalls with piles of fresh mangoes, pineapples, and roasted maize stirred something familiar in her.

'It's terribly unsafe to pack the car here,' Rosina began. Pappi could see what she meant. There were already about a dozen young men peering through the window; three sellers dangling keychains and other items.

'Okay. Drive on and stop over there.' She pointed to the petrol station just down the side street where the crowd was less. Pappi hopped out, clutching her purse, her eyes already drawn past the fruit carts to the cluster of small market stalls just beyond.

As she walked towards them, a memory of herself flushed in her mind, as a little girl walking hand-in-hand between her parents through the market in the Rift Valley. The stall owners, quick to spot her interest, gathered eagerly around her, beckoning her to browse their goods. They spoke over each other, keen for her attention. She bought a few fruits of various kinds, but what truly drew her was the atmosphere, the rhythm of life in these small stalls. It transported her, pulling at something long buried, a piece of her childhood she hadn't realised she'd been yearning for. She hurried back to Rosina's car.

They stopped at the City Market briefly, so that Pappi could see the display of handicrafts.

'You know, I would really like to have those paintings on the walls up the stairway of the old farmhouse.' Pappi said dreamily.

'Wait till next Tuesday. Maasai Market comes into town then, and I will take you there to do your shopping.' Rosina looked at her watch.

'I was thinking - we could stop by my office for a moment. Bernie's been wanting to meet you. After that, the three of us can have lunch at Yaya. I know a really good place there.'

Their office was located in Yaya centre. Rosina worked with Bernie in a publishing firm on the second floor. Bernie carried an easy-going air, dressed in baggy pants and a loose, flowered shirt. He looked like a relaxed tourist, yet at the same time, there was something about him that spoke of an old-time local. They were sitting on the balcony of an Indian restaurant. As the conversation went on Pappi found herself telling them about the cause that had brought her back.

'Throughout the past year I have kept flashing back to Kenya. It was very difficult in the beginning when I felt that this was some-thing I should do – to return back here to help someone that might need help. My experience as an outsider child was my weakness and it was my strength.'

When she finished Bernie said, 'I tried many times to put into words the reason why I decided to live in this country. I think it's precisely why you have returned. The need to do something that could help someone.' Then, like an actor, he lifted his hands in despair and said loudly, 'But what am I doing?' He shook his head as he finally let his hands rest behind it and, stretching his legs out under the table, said, 'I'm publishing books.'

'That's not bad at all,' Pappi began with a serious tone but then she saw the look of hysteria in Rosina's eyes and stopped. Rosina and Bernie laughed.

'Of course it's bad.' Bernie snapped. 'People do not need to read fantasies to escape their disturbed lives.'

'Actually,' Rosina began, now in all seriousness. 'Bernie's plays and articles are often about justice and freedom. He's deeply concerned about the state of this economy.' Pappi knew that. She had read several of his articles, one in Time magazine several months before. They talked some more and with promises of seeing again, she gathered herself into Timotheo's Jeep and let his driver chauffeur her to M.A.T & F.

Chapter 32

Escapades

The company lay on a beautiful plot in Karen, a much quieter location in the suburbs of Nairobi surrounded by farms and homesteads. One got the impression that the company produced yoghurt or cheese. At the gate a guard recognised Timotheo's Jeep and swung the gates open. Pappi stepped out, taking in the nicely done grounds. Here, in this haven, M.A.T & F offered insurance services to companies and many people around the country. It was a spacious white building with big windows. She walked round it, taking in the flower beds, and the handsome trees.

She could see women far away harvesting late maturing crops. Someone was calling out from a distant farm and now she could hear voices shouting responses to each other across farms. She listened and watched. If M.A.T & F had not been there, this might have been a local farm neighbourhood in the 1960s.

'There you are, Miss Pappi. Mr Muriuki is waiting for you in the parlour. Follow me.' Pappi followed Oduor into an airy space in the middle of the building. There was a small coffee shop at the far end where Timotheo sat with a group of men. Now he stood up noisily. 'Pappi my dear!' Then turning to his colleagues, 'Let me introduce you to someone very special, like family to me. We've known each other for decades, and I can honestly say the world is better with her in it.' Polite nods and greetings were said, with genuine curiosity lighting their faces. There were five men and they sat through coffee and tea and a lot of laughter. Finally at five o'clock they stood to leave.

'That's a magnificent building you have there Tim.'

'I'm glad you think so. It's taken twenty years to build it to where it is today. We started in the Industrial Area. Abraham, my business partner, came on board fifteen years ago - brought real wisdom with him.'

'Younger businessman?' Pappi asked, intrigued.

'Fresh out of college, almost,' Timotheo chuckled, a hint of pride in his voice.

Pappi's eyebrows lifted in genuine surprise. 'Tim, I'm impressed! Bringing someone that young into the heart of your business - that takes vision.'

'Or desperation.'

'How so?'

'Well, we weren't exactly flying high back then. The company needed fresh eyes. Abraham knew things I didn't even know I needed to know.'

'It takes a big man to share the reins with someone young enough to be your own child.' Pappi said with admiration.

Tim nodded, his eyes thoughtful. 'He was Rosina's suitor for some time. Now I do not know what will happen to Rosie. She's not getting any younger.'

'She's still young. You'll see. When the right man comes along, Rosie will be swept off her feet in no time.' She was trying to cheer him up because suddenly he had sulked and sat there looking straight ahead.

'I offered her a good position at the company. A solid job, room to grow, all the right people around her. She would have thrived there. But no, she turned it down.' He shook his head with a mix of frustration. 'She chose instead to publish articles. She says it's where her heart is.'

'Perhaps she's building something you can't see yet.'

'I still think she's throwing away golden opportunities, but then again, maybe that's what I would have done at her age.'

'She's your daughter,' Pappi said measuredly. 'Somewhere along the line she must have learnt from you to follow her heart.'

'Well, I suppose I can't argue with that.' He rubbed the back of his neck, his eyes briefly distant, then turned and smiled at Pappi.

Dinner was usually between six and seven in Muriuki's home, so when they arrived the table was already laid and Njoki sat there beside the fire knitting as she listened and occasionally commented on what her guest was saying. Her guest was a woman who lived on a nearby farm. She had dropped in with produce from her farm - sweet potatoes and arrowroots. Now they both exclaimed something joyfully when they saw Timotheo and Pappi.

They had a sumptuous dinner of white beans, fried arrowroots, french beans fried with carrots, and chicken. Muthoni had squeezed two litres of mango juice, which was over by the end of dinner. Afterwards they said goodbye to Njoki's friend, and settled into the living room. Tim leaned back, his arm draped loosely over the side of his chair. 'So, Pappi, you've returned at an interesting time. The country feels lighter, somehow. Like we're finally breathing out.'

'The elections certainly stirred something, even from afar.' Pappi said with a broad smile.

'You're right. People believe again.' Njoki said.

Tim nodded, thoughtful. 'President Kibaki has inspired a kind of hope I haven't seen in decades. Still I can't help wondering if the weight of the old guard won't creep back in.'

'Optimism may be risky business,' Pappi said gently, 'but perhaps it's the most essential kind of courage.'

'Speaking of courage,' Njoki said, 'You're very bold in planning to move back to your old home!'

Pappi laughed lightly, 'most of the time I am wondering if I know what I am up against.' She said, 'It may be unfinished business that's driving me. That land remembers me, even if I've forgotten parts of myself.'

'Going back is about making peace with something.' Timotheo said, standing up to make a drink.

'Tim tells me your house is starting to come together.' Njoki said.

'So I hear! I can't wait to see it for myself soon.'

'The new roof is on,' Timotheo assured, 'and they're almost done with the work inside. I believe you will be pleasantly surprised.'

'That house holds so many layers of me. I wonder if I will recognize myself in it.'

'You'll find more of yourself there than you expect,' Tim said quietly. 'Places are patient like that. They don't change, no matter how much we do.'

The following day was Saturday, and Njoki had a work event in town. Pappi took her breakfast on the veranda. Her project idea lay spread before her on the table in various coloured notebooks and loose papers: *children in informal settlements unable to attend school; mothers without basic skills or access to steady income; teenage boys huddling in idle groups, with zero exposure to mentorship or tools for the modern world.* And then of course, *teenage mothers.* The needs were vast. Yet the complexity of it all gave Pappi purpose.

By late morning, she had made three phone calls to individuals that friends had connected her with - a social worker who ran a successful community feeding program in Mathare; a woman named Eunice who oversaw a small vocational centre for girls in Kibera; and an education officer working within a private foundation focused on digital literacy in under-resourced schools. All had agreed to meet her the following week.

Chapter 33

Momentum

At the end of the third week, she spent time drafting a framework, which she sent to Chris for review. He called her.

'It's good,' he said, 'but you'd be firing on all cylinders without much impact. Let's narrow it down.' They worked closely over the phone, creating an approach: listen first, learn, and then build together. They sorted through the needs and possibilities. 'Start where the lines cross,' he said. 'What do you mean?' 'Where multiple problems touch the same people. Like young mothers - they're caring for children, they lack income, and they may never have finished school. If we start there, we're addressing education, livelihoods, and childcare in one place.'

They agreed that the initial focus would be on teenage and young mothers, those raising children in slum areas. They listed the categories of need, as a way to frame the future growth of the project: *Education Access* for both children and mothers, basic literacy, school enrolment, and opportunities to complete unfinished education. *Livelihood & Vocational Skills* - practical training linked to local economies, helping women and youth earn income with dignity. *Mentorship & Mental Well-being* - structured guidance and emotional support, particularly for teenagers who were drifting without direction. *Nutrition & Early Childhood Development* - reliable access to food, and support systems for young children and their caregivers. *Digital & Future Skills* - computer literacy, communication, and creative tools that could break generational cycles of poverty.

By Monday morning of January 27, Pappi had circled the first two as a starting point. She met Eunice that afternoon at her Centre, located between narrow alleys and corrugated roofs. Girls were learning tailoring, basic accounting, and spoken English. 'What we need now,' Eunice said, 'is a link to the outside. Someone who can help us grow, beyond just survival.'

On Wednesday, Pappi met the tech educator, Davie, at a small café near Westlands. He was young and full of ideas. 'There's a generation of bright kids who don't need charity - they need access,' he was saying, 'and they need someone who believes they're worth the effort.'

By Friday, Pappi had filled an entire new notebook. In the late afternoon, Rosina called to check on her, and gave a casual invitation to come over. She drove up within an hour to pick her up. The weather was nice and warm, and the heat never rose beyond twenty five degrees, which was unusual for January. Rosina was dressed in sleek gym leggings, a fitted tank top, and trainers. Her hair was tied back in a neat puff, and a water bottle rolled at her feet as she opened the car door.

Pappi smiled as she stepped in. 'Well, you look like someone who's either just finished conquering the world - or about to.'

Rosina laughed. 'Neither. The only sport I do is run up and down my flight of stairs.'

'Dressed for gym?'

Rosina shrugged, 'It helps me feel closer to my goal.'

'Well. Whatever gets you to your goal.' They laughed.

'Good meetings behind?' Rosina asked.

Pappi told Rosina about the meetings she'd had that week, and the unexpected phone call from the secretary of the MP for the Rift Valley region who was a friend of Timotheo's, and who sounded eager to collaborate.

'They're hoping you'll help him deliver on his campaign promises,' Rosina said with a wry smile. 'Like creating jobs.'

Pappi glanced at her. 'Isn't that a worthy goal?'

Rosina shrugged. 'Of course it is. Just don't let anyone use you to tick boxes or polish their image. Politicians are rarely as interested in long-term change.'

Pappi nodded thoughtfully. 'Fair point. But I do trust your dad's judgment. And it's not the politician I'm chasing. It's the people on the ground. If his office opens doors to real work, I'm willing to walk through.'

Rosina smiled. 'Good. Just promise me you'll keep your eyes open.'

'I will,' Pappi assured her.

Her thoughts drifted to Njoro. She was eager to see the place again, and to meet the locals. A good connection there could unlock a network of support she couldn't build alone. Timotheo had set up a proper digital security system back in December as advised by Chris, because she planned to base her work at the old homestead.

They had lunch at one of the restaurants in the Village Market, borrowed a movie for the evening, did some grocery shopping and then they drove to Rosina's home. Rosina had seventeen year old triplets who were away at boarding school.

'How do you cope with them away so many months in a year?' Pappi asked. She couldn't imagine ever having sent Elizabeth to a boarding school. Rosina was up and down the kitchen, trying to fix a dinner that they'd be eating three hours later.

'I keep busy. It's just the way here, all their friends are in boarding schools.' Then she paused. 'But I get super happy when they're coming back.'

'I can only imagine.' Pappi smiled.

'When they were little they almost lived with my parents. I was a workaholic, and I loved to be on the move. It was easier to just dump them on mom and dad and take days doing nonstop work.'

'I'm sure your parents didn't mind.' Pappi said encouragingly.

'I know. But I was a bad mom.'

'Come on now,' Pappi squeezed her hand, which had stopped chopping cucumbers as she contemplated. 'Look, you've been a mother and a father to these children, and that is a hard thing to be, especially when you have three of them.'

'But I could have been a better mom.' She resumed her chopping, and Pappi could tell she had things in her mind. When Rosina didn't continue she said firmly, 'Don't be hard on yourself.'

'How about you?' Rosina asked after a while. 'Didn't you want to have more children?'

'No. Elizabeth was enough for me.' Pappi said softly. 'Between work, studying, and everything in between, I barely kept my head above water.'

Rosina glanced at her. 'Sometimes I wondered what life would have been like if you'd married uncle Michael, and never left.'

Pappi thought for a moment. Then she said, 'Marriage was never on our minds. Besides, I have always loved Chris. I am sure I would have found my way to him.'

She picked up a peeler and started with the carrots, peeling away as they moved to lighter conversations. They were driving up the next morning to a children's home, where Rosina would be donating clothes and Pappi would be spending the day meeting the children.

Chapter 34

Inconsistencies

Pappi was becoming more and more accustomed to life in Nairobi. On several occasions, she had insisted on taking the *matatu* from Ngong Hills to the city centre, wanting to experience the city as most did. She made a trip to the Rift Valley in the first few days of February, and stayed at the farmhouse which was now fully reno- vated after weeks of delay. The water system had been the great- est challenge - outdated pipes, faulty drainage - but at Chris's firm urging, she had finally agreed to have the entire network replaced.

She was at Rosina's, where they had just had dinner and said goodbye to Bernie. He would be travelling to Botswana the follow- ing day to finish a documentary he had been working on. Rosina and Pappi were watching the 9 o'clock news.

'What if I told you that I think dad had something to do with Alex's disappearance?'

Pappi stared at the screen, then she turned to her, 'Why would you say a thing like that?'

Rosina sat facing her on the couch. 'When I got pregnant with the triplets dad was distraught. Neither of them had liked Alex but secretly I think mom was happy about my pregnancy. Having grandchildren would almost replace my brother.' Pappi propped her legs up on the couch, took a cushion and hugged it.

Alex moved through Nairobi University campus with a quiet confidence that made people instinctively take notice. He did not seek attention yet there was something magnetic about him and he had students around him regularly. He excelled in political theory where his essays were known for their sharp analysis and surprising originality, yet he rarely engaged in debates unless directly challenged. When he did speak, he often dismantled arguments, not to win, but to reveal the flaws in uninformed thinking. Most of the people Alex admired were long-dead revolutionaries, men who had fought for justice with fire in their bellies and ideas that outlived them. He read widely - Achebe, Frantz Fanon, Thomas Sankara, Baldwin, Camus - and quoted them to ground his views on economics and politics. Among his living heroes, there was one figure Alex held in equal esteem: Justus Muriuki. Muriuki embodied the kind of moral clarity and strategic brilliance that Alex envied. His application to study at the University of Nairobi had been calculated. He knew that Muriuki's granddaughter, Rosina, was also enrolled there, and he intended to win her over as a way to get close to the man himself. He pursued her with charm and although he hadn't expected Rosina to be the mother of his children, he couldn't think of a better future than the one she'd usher him into.

'I knew little of Alex's past. He was a student at the University and we had some similar lectures. He wanted to be a businessman of some sort. He had lots of friends. That was something I never had, and my world changed when I met him. It was easy to see that everyone in his circles listened to him. Usually they were on the move a lot. They seemed to be involved in business somewhere, and Alex was often travelling to various towns. I stopped questioning him at some point. But when I got pregnant and my parents threw me out,'

'Wait. Who threw you out?' Pappi asked, perplexed.

'Dad couldn't handle it, that I was pregnant.'

'Rosie, I had no idea. That must have been tough!'

'Well, dad likes things to stay perfect. *We've got many eyes on us*, he used to say. Mistakes like that were just too conspicuous.'

'What happened?'

'One day, in November just before the final examinations were over Alex failed to pick me up. I knew something was wrong.'

'Didn't you reach out to someone? Your uncle?'

Rosina shook her head. 'Uncle Michael is worse than dad.'

She paused, looking at the TV screen. 'The next day, one of Alex's friends came to the apartment and said Alex had been in an accident. He wanted to see me. He took me to a house in Thika, where Alex was recovering.'

'What happened to him?' Pappi asked impatiently.

'They said he'd been in a car accident. But the kind of hurt he had - it wasn't from a car accident. He'd been beaten. I told him he needed a hospital, but he dismissed it.'

Rosina went quiet for a moment. Pappi tried to process what she was hearing.

In early 1985, Alex's carefully constructed world began to unravel. One evening, as he drove through a quiet part of Nairobi, he realized he was being followed. Moments later, he was ambushed by unknown men, dragged from his car, beaten with ruthless efficiency, and given a warning. Days later, the message became clearer when Rosina's uncle, a high-ranking government official with ties to intelligence networks, summoned him in secret. He offered Alex a hefty sum of money, enough to disappear comfortably. If Alex didn't leave the country immediately and sever all contact with Rosina, the next encounter wouldn't end with bruises. Alex understood the language of violence well enough, having been raised by his uncle, Doctor Jon. Within a week, he vanished without a trace, leaving Rosina with no explanation, and a silence that would haunt her for years.

'It wasn't long after that and he just vanished.'

'You must have been devastated,' Pappi said gently.

'Hollowed out.' Rosina said, exhaling as though she'd been holding her breath.

Her parents had taken her back in. They adored the children and helped care for them. But Rosina herself was in no state to function. Two years passed like that. Then, when the fog began to lift, Rosina decided to search for answers. She drove back to the flat that she and Alex had once shared. The new tenants had no idea who Alex was. An elderly neighbour remembered movers clearing out the apartment shortly after Rosina had left. But she never saw Alex.

'I had been so isolated,' She continued. 'Alex's friends had dispersed, and of course I did not have their phone numbers. Nor addresses. But I remembered the house in Thika, so I drove there.'

'Well?' Pappi probed.

'The same couple and a few young people in their twenties still lived in the house. They said my father had paid Alex to disappear.'

'That's a bit of a stretch!'

'Oh you don't know my father, or uncle Michael.' Rosina walked to the window, drew the curtains, stopping for a moment to peer into the night. Pappi shivered. A memory stirred - of that week after the 1963 New Year's party in the barn. She remembered the feeling of safety inside the barn amongst her friends. Yet the insecure nagging, not knowing what would happen the day after. Would they all be gone, to safe havens around the world, leaving her to battle her identities? She looked at the curtains, now shut, feeling safe again.

Rosina returned to the couch. 'Whether or not Alex was threatened remains a mystery, but he took the offer anyway and vanished.'

A movie was playing on TV. The Titanic was going down, passengers screaming, the band playing *'Nearer, My God, To Thee'* as water swallowed the decks. Pappi sat still, watching the chaos unfold on screen, and thought, *Is there a world where people are just plain safe?* She glanced at Rosina, a thousand questions quietly turning in her mind.

'It's shocking.' Pappi managed. Rosina knew how close Pappi was with her parents, and had considered that Pappi might find it difficult to believe her. Strangely, as difficult as it was to take in, Pappi did not doubt Rosina.

'Did you ever discuss this with your parents?' She asked.

'With the man who paid my children's dad to vanish out of their lives?' Rosina went to the kitchen to find the half-full bottle of Mâcon-Villages, the crisp white Burgundy she'd picked up from a distributor near Hurlingham. She returned with two glasses, handed one to Pappi, who set it on the table.

'This is very difficult, Rosina. I don't understand how you have managed to keep this inside for so long. Speak to your dad.'

'I'm not ready to do that.'

They sat there in silence.

'You need to speak to your dad, Rosina.' Pappi said firmly, 'There has to be an explanation, if all this is true.'

Chapter 35

Unravelling Secrets

Pappi and Njoki drove in silence along the winding road that led them back to Ngong Hills. The sun had begun its descent towards the horizon, casting long shadows as it descended, and a gentle breeze rustled through the open windows of the car. There was a warm glow over the landscape, which was dotted with acacia trees. The baskets from the Juja market lay in the backseat. Pappi was thinking of the long conversation they'd had the last few days with Njoki, Timotheo, and Rosina. Without waiting for a second prompting, Rosina had asked her father whether he'd been involved in Alex's disappearance. Pappi wondered how she had drawn herself into this intricate web of family secrets. The revelation that Rosina suspected her own father's involvement in Alex's disappearance made it impossible for Pappi to stay detached, though now she wished she had remained ignorant of the truth.

Timotheo had admitted to having paid Alex to leave the country, effectively orchestrating his departure from Rosina's life. He recounted the desperate measures he had taken to protect his daughter from what he had believed was a potentially dangerous relationship. Michael had found out about Alex's involvement in ivory trafficking, and had planned his escape from imprisonment if he promised to leave the country. Rosina had sat in stunned silence.

'Mom, did you know?' She had asked.

Njoki nodded, too ashamed to speak. Rosina felt betrayed, yet oddly relieved that there had been a bigger, if painful, reason. Perhaps even a form of protection for her and her children. The past days had been an emotional rollercoaster for all of them, and Pappi felt utterly powerless. She longed for London. For the familiar faces in her life - her own family, Chris, Mary-Anne. Even Patrick.

She broke the silence. 'Picking up these baskets was a great idea, Njoki. They'll be perfect for the bazaar.'

Njoki nodded, her eyes focused on the winding road. 'Yes, they are quite unique. People always appreciate handmade crafts like these. And the artisans in Juja are so talented.'

Pappi examined one of the baskets, running her fingers along the woven patterns. 'I remember when I used to visit the market place in Nakuru as a child with my parents. The market is one of my fondest memories.'

Njoki smiled. 'I have fond memories of exploring the markets with my mother and sisters as well. The good thing about marketplaces is that they have retained their charm over the years.'

Pappi's eyes sparkled with nostalgia. 'True! The aroma of street foods, the colourful fabrics. It's like stepping back in time.' A soft laugh escaped from both.

'Pappi. Thank you for helping Rosina through all this mess. What we did was wrong.'

'No family is perfect.' Pappi looked at Njoki as she drove. 'And what happened is in the past now.'

They shared stories of their childhood, weaving their memories into the present moment. She'd been staying with Njoki and Timotheo for a month now. And so much had happened. She remembered Chris' firm comment after the revelation of Alex's disappearance. 'Paps, listen carefully. I want you to move to a hotel. Muriuki's family clearly has issues they must deal with, and you mustn't be caught in between.' But Timotheo had called him back when she mentioned she'd be moving to a nearby hotel.

'The thing is that she's already so involved now.' Then more somberly, 'I can't apologise enough Chris, for getting her into this mess. But I promise you, we're cleaning up our mess, and we're taking care of her.'

Njoki navigated the narrow roads with ease, her hands steady on the wheel. They approached their destination. Timotheo and Njoki's house was a harmonious blend of contemporary design and traditional Kenyan elements. The house's exterior featured a combination of earthy tones that complemented the natural surroundings of the area. Large windows allowed ample light to flood the interior, providing breathtaking views of the beautiful large lawn outside. The roof, made of locally sourced materials, had a unique, sloping design that added character to the house.

The living room was tastefully decorated with African art and crafts, reflecting the rich cultural diversity of Kenya. Wooden furnishings and toned down earthy palettes created a welcoming and cosy atmosphere. The bazaar would be held in a matter of days, in the beautiful lawn behind the house.

Chapter 36

The Bazaar

Njoki darted between tables piled high with handicrafts. She wore vibrant African prints and had a swirl of energy. 'Pappi, darling, you wouldn't believe how much money has already started flowing in from the guests that can't make it.' She flashed a radiant smile, feeling purposeful. Though there had been several cancellations, they all came with apologies and generous donations.

Pappi gracefully adjusted a row of hand-painted vases. Her heart was racing, not just from the excitement of the event but also because Chris was finally here.

Njoki said playfully, watching her, 'Ah, Chris! I swear, I can see hearts in your eyes every time you're thinking of him.'

Pappi rolled her eyes. 'Nonsense! I've no time for thoughts,' she lied. Njoki shook her head, her curls dancing like tendrils. 'You're a terrible liar darling. He's written all over your face.' She grinned at Pappi. 'And he's right behind you.'

'Pappillote.'

She turned, threw herself into his embrace. 'You haven't called me that since I was 10.' He held her, thinking how lucky he was. He was transported back to the old farmhouse where Pappi lived with her parents. It was a humble home compared to many other homes in their community, but it was where many adults came for soul healing. He remembered the day he'd carried her from his dad's truck, setting her on the couch in their living room, her ankle already swollen.

Chris pulled her away and looked at her. 'I'm glad you never changed it.'

'What?'

'Your beautiful name. I'm glad you kept it.'

Growing up she had hated her name. It had been a basis for bullying when there was no other way for kids to get to her. She had said many times that once she was old enough she would change her name. She smiled back at him, 'I'm glad I didn't change it.'

'Put those in a jar?' Njoki winked. Pappi looked at the roses in her hands, shouted back, 'Oh no. These are going to my room.' She walked into the house, noticing the time. In two hours the house would be buzzing with guests.

The bazaar was finally underway, and the atmosphere was filled with excitement. Guests arrived dressed in fine attire, and the venue was beautifully adorned for the occasion. Patrick and Timotheo greeted the guests warmly, the hired waiters behind them offering a selection of drinks and delicious starters. Moving silently through the crowd, they ensured everyone had a glass of champagne or a refreshing cocktail in hand.

At the back door Pappi and Chris stood on the veranda, their faces lit up with warm smiles as they engaged in friendly and casual conversations with the guests. Pappi was dressed elegantly in a flowing, emerald-green gown. The gown's delicate sequin shimmered later in the evening, under the soft lighting, and her heavy curls fell just above her shoulders in untamed disarray. She wore a simple necklace and matching earrings to add a touch of sophistication to her look. Chris wore a tailored charcoal-grey suit. His crisp white dress shirt impeccably ironed, the top two buttons undone to convey casual elegance.

A small stir rippled through the crowd as Justus Muriuki, Recipient of Head Of State Commendation, arrived. As he entered the venue, polite applause and murmurs of recognition followed him. The pristine and neatly manicured lawn was now a hive of activity. At the far end of the large compound, stalls were draped in Kenyan traditional products providing shopping opportunities, with all proceeds going to support the project. The centre of the green expanse had a large white tent under which were tables and chairs, each table with different centrepiece flowers such as roses, orchids, African lily, and the Kikuyu white lily. Mary-Anne and Njoki guided guests to their assigned seats.

Chapter 37

A Noble Cause

Justus Muriuki stood to make his keynote speech. The guests clapped as the eighty-two year old rose to his feet, many aware of his vital yet behind-the-scenes role in the country's struggle for independence. His legal training and extensive networks had supported men who led the nation to freedom, many of whom never lived to see it.

He wore a warm and approachable quality about him, and conveyed genuine enthusiasm for the initiative they had all gathered for.

'I stand here not as a man seeking applause, but as a witness to the power of enduring hope and of collective effort. I look at you all - your belief in something larger than yourselves - and I see the very foundation of our nation's future being completed. A loud applause. He waved his hand for silence, and continued.

Some say that great change comes from great leaders. I disagree. I have long believed that it comes from ordinary people choosing, day after day, to show up and to build, precept after precept. Clapping erupted from the crowd. He waved his hand again.

I've seen what it takes to rebuild after struggle. During our fight for independence, we learned that freedom means nothing if it does not lift everyone. What you're doing here today is exactly that lifting. Your support for this project will be transformative. You may not see the results tomorrow. But rest assured, you have set in motion something that matters.

The audience stood up clapping.

Roger had slipped quietly into the crowd during Justus's speech. Many in the audience were familiar with his contributions to research, particularly during his tenure at the University of Nairobi. He was an accomplished scholar whose work played a significant part in the development in Kenya.

The night was filled with a sense of accomplishment as the bazaar drew to a close. The guests began to disperse, coming up to thank Pappi. Small groups still sat down at tables, or stood, drinking and talking. She stood amidst the remnants of the successful event.

'Paps darling,' Mary-Anne stepped out, now dressed in her flowery dress coat. She kissed her on both cheeks. 'What a great success. And the professor's speech was very moving,' Pappi agreed, feeling a quiet relief. She had originally thought to invite one of last year's presidential candidates to speak, but plans had shifted. In the end, she was genuinely grateful that Justus had agreed to deliver the keynote. His reputation and steady presence had brought a sense of trust to the event.

'You must be exhausted,' she said to Mary-Anne, looking her over. 'Thank you for taking care of the guests tonight.'

'I enjoyed every moment,' She looked over at Njoki, who was now making her way to them. 'She's the one that's exhausted, dancing as she did all night. And quite the chatterbox.'

'Speak for yourself,' Njoki said, a bit tipsy from the wine. 'And why you insist on staying at a hotel when there are enough rooms here, I don't know.' Patrick came to fetch Mary-Anne and the two left. Oduor would drive them to their hotel and bring them the next day for a late breakfast.

They retired in the late night into Timotheo's den, where he served drinks to Chris and Roger. Njoki had gone straight to bed. Pappi, a cup of hot chocolate cuddled in her hands, sat at the reclining chair near the fireplace, where there was no fire. Her thoughts were running wild. So far she had a team of ten, each bringing their unique skills to the table. Building strong partnerships and collaborations as she did tonight was key to the success of the project. Njoki had taken the responsibility to mobilise the international community that she worked with and local NGOs, and Timotheo had taken charge of government agencies to create a strong network of support.

Her thoughts turned to the mothers and children, who would benefit from these efforts. She imagined safe and nurturing environments, educational opportunities, and healthcare provisions that would help them thrive. But she had no clue how all these would come together.

Chapter 38

The Old Farmhouse

The descent into the Great Rift Valley was as dramatic as they all remembered. As their vehicle wound down from Nairobi's escarpments, the land opened wide before them, rolling hills and flat plains stretching to the horizon. It was 11am when they stopped at the Rift Valley escarpment viewpoint near *Mai Mahiu,* to have a look at Lake Naivasha. The vendors were busy at work, having arrived as early as 7 to catch early travellers. They continued their drive, the shimmer of the lake fading behind them. In the distance, patches of cultivated farmland now broke the once-uninterrupted savannah. Where acacia trees had once stood in isolation, houses now filled the spaces. They drove quietly, taking the change all in.

The tarmac road beneath them had replaced the old dusty tracks they had all known in their youth. Towns that were once sleepy outposts now bustled with life - motorbikes zipped by, children in school uniforms chased each other along the roadside, and kiosks sold everything from mangoes to mobile phone airtime. Billboards advertising soda and mobile networks punctuated the scenery, evidence of a country now rooted in the 21st century.

The house stood distinctly against the crude village surroundings. It was now painted white. The farm looked both familiar and different, frozen in time yet bearing the marks of years gone by. The woody acacia tree, with its thick branches spread out, stood as Chris remembered it, just outside the house. Its bark bore the marks of countless seasons, each crevice and furrow telling age-old stories. The trunk, thick and gnarled, conveyed a sense of ancient wisdom.

'Weird,' Pappi whispered, as she looked at the tree.

'What's weird?' Njoki asked, following her gaze up the tree.

'It's as though it was left behind,' she said, 'This tree. It's the only thing that looks exactly the same as it did then.'

The leaves rustled in the breeze. Njoki looked at Pappi, 'Sometimes I wish I'd understand what Kenya looks like from your perspective.'

Pappi laughed. 'I envy you, you know.' She said as they walked to the house.

'Whatever for?' Njoki laughed.

'Well, you know what your roots are.'

For Chris, the house appeared much smaller than he remembered. The memories of his time here made him feel slightly disoriented. Roger slapped him on the shoulder, letting his hand rest there.

'Getting sentimental, Chris?'

'Aren't you? It feels like a snapshot of the past. Except that the exterior of the house is now modern white.'

They walked to the barn, where Timotheo was now jerking the double doors open. Cobwebs deterred him from going right in. He tried to see through the webs.

'So, lads! This was the hub of youthful exuberance?' He chuckled.

'And secret rendezvous,' Grinned Roger. 'You should have seen the lot of us'

The barn now stood as a weathered and run-down structure. It was a reminder of the passage of time and the changes in between. Roger was telling Timotheo about their teenage escapades, and about the day they almost burned it down. Chris was retracing moments they had shared in the barn. It held a special significance for him, and it was here that he had formed some of the most profound connections in his life.

The contents in the barn were mostly things from Pappi's farmhouse. As the three men stepped into the dimly lit space, they were struck by the musty scent of history that hung in the air. Their eyes scanned the interior, taking in the old furniture, some of it ornate and antique, that stood in various corners. There were wooden chairs with intricately carved backs and a table with worn but elegant designs, now covered in dust.

A big wooden box was tucked away in a corner. Pappi had mentioned it once, a repository of treasures from her parents' house that she couldn't bear to part with. Chris opened the lid, blew away a thick layer of dust from the items on top. Among the items were sepia-toned photographs capturing moments from Pappi's childhood, with her parents and friends. A collection of vintage books, their pages yellowed, lined the box.

Timotheo stood watching the two men as they went through the items.

'I wonder if Paps will want to keep any of these things,' Chris said thoughtfully.

'Every item here holds a piece of her heritage. I reckon she will want to keep it all as long as it's not broken.' Roger said, placing a hand again on Chris's shoulder. They walked towards the house.

Mary-Anne and Patrick had gone on a walk just after arriving, down the road that led to the estate that once belonged to Mary-Anne's family. As they reached the spot where the grand estate lay, they were met with an entirely different landscape. The sprawling land that Mary-Anne once knew was now a patchwork of smaller farms, each with its own houses and cultivated land. Her parents had sold the land back in 1963, and evidently it had been divided and sold to several farmers over the years.

She gazed at the transformed site, melancholy washing over her. Their family house, once a handsome and stoic structure perched on higher ground than the rest of the estate, now stood with hunched shoulders, its paint faded and, to Mary-Anne's astonishment, the elevated ground on which it stood appeared to have levelled out. Nothing was as she remembered. She whispered to Patrick as they walked back to Pappi's farm hand-in-hand, 'It's so different now, Pat. I can hardly recognize it.'

Patrick looked around with a sense of wonder as they walked. He kissed her hand and said, 'Yes, it must be different, but there's something beautiful about the way life continues to flourish. Look at these children for instance.' They waved and smiled at the group of children who had stopped playing the moment the vehicle drove up, and who had followed Mary-Anne and Patrick down the road. They looked happy and carefree as ever. Mary-Anne said to them, '*Hamjambo!*' And they roared with laughter. The tallest one of them answered, '*Hatujambo!*'

They stopped at the old barn, its weathered wooden walls captivating Patrick, who had always been fascinated by the charm of rural life. The men had left the doors ajar, and they peeked in. A small smile tugged at the corners of Mary-Anne's lips, 'Now this is home,' she said.

Pappi appeared at the door of the main house, 'What kept you? Come on in, we'll start dinner soon.' She was holding her phone with one hand, and resumed a conversation with Sue.

As they stepped into the renovated house, Mary-Anne gasped in amazement. The transformation was nothing short of breathtaking. It was a spacious, light-filled space that retained the warmth of history, like the candle-lit chandelier which hung from the kitchen ceiling. Her parent's ornate grandfather clock was against one wall, and the grand piano stood magnificently against another wall.

The centrepiece of the dining area was the old, beautifully crafted antique table. Its now polished surface still bore the marks of countless dinners. The refurbished fireplace, and the well-worn wooden beams in the ceiling were a piece of the past. Mary-Anne couldn't contain her awe as she entered the living room which was transformed into open space. The walls to the kitchen and to what used to be Pappi's father's den had been removed, creating a seamless flow between the living room and kitchen. 'Wow,' she exclaimed, her eyes wide. 'It's so airy!'

Roger nodded in agreement. 'Like a whole new house.'

The large glass panels framed the stunning view of the farm in a way that felt like bringing the outside inside. Pappi was beaming, her arms around Chris. She had wanted to preserve the essence of the house, while giving it a fresh start, and she was happy at how well the work was done.

'You've done an amazing job with the place, Paps.' Mary-Anne swirled around, taking it all in.

'Thanks to Timotheo and his renovating team.' Pappi said, disentangling herself from Chris' arms.

Roger strolled over to the antique cabinet in the dining area, his eyes scanning the well-organised collection of glassware. He carefully selected enough glasses for everyone. With theatrical grace, He uncorked a bottle of Sancerre, pouring into each glass. Turning to face his friends, who now had a glass in hand each, he raised his glass. 'Thank you Tim, for bringing Pappi's house alive. To transformations,' he declared.

'To transformations,' they echoed in unison. Patrick, feeling a deep sense of belonging said, 'No matter how much things change, some things remain constant. Like friendships.' Harmonious nods affirmed their mutual agreement.

'Very well said,' Timotheo exclaimed, putting his glass down and clasping his hands. 'The sun is beginning its descent, gentlemen, and barbecue awaits!' They swiftly divided into two groups to tackle different aspects of the meal, the men heading outside after Timotheo, to chop wood and prepare the outdoor fireplace.

Inside the cosy farmhouse kitchen, the women took charge of dressing the chicken and preparing the other meats destined for the grill. Mary-Anne's nimble fingers expertly seasoned the cuts of meat. Njoki took charge of the greens, skillfully chopping and mixing a medley of fresh vegetables. The salad would perfectly complement the smoky flavours of the barbecue.

They gathered on the glassed porch as the night descended upon the farm. The dimly lit interior revealed a table beautifully set, with the perfectly grilled meat, salads, and different kinds of sauces. The soft glow of candles added an intimate ambiance, creating an inviting atmosphere.

Outside the glassed porch, the embers of the barbecue fire glowed. Timotheo had promised to ensure it was fully extinguished before they went to bed. When dinner concluded, the group migrated indoors to the living room. They settled, glasses of their favourite drinks in hand, now engaged in conversations that spanned from the mundane to the profound, with occasional loud laughters. Chris had carried a small golden ball in his pocket all evening, waiting for the perfect moment to seize his future with Pappi.

When he knelt down before Pappi the room fell silent. 'My love,' he began, 'from the moment I met you, you've shown me the beauty of life, the strength of love, and the power of hope.'

Pappi's heart raced, realising what was happening. Chris continued, 'In this golden ball,' he said, opening it slowly to reveal a delicate diamond ring, 'I hold a symbol of the love and commitment I feel for you. My darling Paps, will you marry me and make me the happiest man in the whole world?'

The room held its breath. Pappi's eyes glistened and she nodded, 'Yes! Of course I'll marry you!' She held out her hand, and Chris slipped the diamond ring onto her finger.

Chapter 39

The Party in the Barn

The morning air drifted with the familiar smell of rural life. The narrow village road filled quickly with unexpected traffic, cars hooting impatiently as they inched past slow-moving tractors hauling produce. A dusty pickup truck, piled high with sugarcane, had stalled briefly, creating a traffic jam. Boda boda riders weaved through gaps with practiced ease.

News about Chris and Pappi's engagement rippled through their circle of friends and family. Elizabeth immediately began making plans to travel to Kenya to join in the preparations.

'Elizabeth darling, as we are having it rather soon, perhaps you want to come for the wedding, and leave the preparations part for me and the others here?'

'Mom!' Elizabeth scolded, 'Are you trying to keep me from the best part of the wedding?'

'Of course not darling!' The truth of the matter was, Pappi couldn't wait to see her daughter and grandchildren. And Jason. So they gladly settled. 'Come, as soon as possible.'

Across the Atlantic Ocean, Sue wasted no time booking a flight to Kenya, eager to take over the wedding preparations. She was determined to make the wedding day as special and memorable as possible for Chris and Pappi. The ceremony was scheduled for the end of March, a small intimate affair with only closest friends and family in attendance. Pappi couldn't have it any other way.

She thought of her parents. In a quiet corner of England, in a care home for the elderly. Her father had gone senile, now in his mid nineties. Her mother, though 92, was still sharp in her mind and determined to witness her daughter's wedding.

Pappi thought of the agonising years of her teens, the opposition by her parents. Now as she prepared to marry Chris, her heart ached for her parents. They had not known any better, both raised in strict conservative homes and knowing nothing but segregation. She did not know what to do about her mother, who insisted on being brought to Njoro for the wedding. She had tried to convince her that she could watch the wedding on video.

'Absolutely not,' her mother said firmly. 'This wedding will be a moment of reconciliation. I must be there.'

Pappi felt a lump in her throat. 'And closure.' She quietly said. 'It's also a moment of closure, mother.'

'Yes, Pappilotte. Love has prevailed.'

Chris wanted to bring Pappi's vision of the wedding of her dreams to life, and went about transforming the barn into the perfect party place. With the help of Roger, George the watchman, and a few skilled local craftsmen, they worked tirelessly to create a tasteful setting.

Elizabeth arrived first, along with her family and Pappi's mother. Pappi had hired a driver to pick them up at the airport and drive them to the Rift Valley. As the car came to a stop, she rushed down the steps and into the driveway, embracing everyone as they spilled out of the Nissan. She assisted her mother out of the car, a small and petite figure, and happier than Pappi had ever seen her.

'My Pappilotte.' She said as she embraced her.

'I can't believe you're here, mother.' They walked into the house, but not before Pappi's mother turned to have a look at the barn. She was holding onto a walking stick, and she now lifted it and aimed it at the barn.

'Don't you think I do not know what went on in there.' She said, a mischievous look in her eyes. Pappi laughed, helping her into the house.

The rest arrived a week before the wedding and joined immediately in the preparations. The men carried the grand piano out into the barn and Linda practised every night after they were done with fixing things. The farmhouse had gradually evolved into lively excitement and since they could not all fit in the house, the men pitched tents in the compound.

On the day of the wedding, a self-serve breakfast was laid out on the porch for everyone to enjoy at their leisure. The cooks now dominated the kitchen, putting together a feast that mirrored the day's significance. The wedding ceremony would be in the evening, giving everyone a chance to unwind. Outside, the barn had been beautifully transformed, the winding pathway in the compound lined with lanterns and flowers, and the acacia tree dressed with fairy lights. They had just finished fixing the fairy lights and Chris was standing on a ladder about to descend.

'I'll be in Kenya often over the next months, bud, happy to come up here,' Roger was saying, 'if you need me for any relational counselling. I might be useful that way.' He winked at Chris. Chris laughed, stepping off the ladder. 'For a couple that's known each other forever?'

'You're like the oldest married couple around here,' Tony chuckled, shaking his head as he picked up a toolbox and headed for the house.

'Say Chris,' started Greg. He was crouched by the boxes under the tree, putting everything back that they wouldn't be using. 'What kept you from getting to the altar sooner?'

'Paps needed time. None of us can imagine what it was like growing up with the lot of us.'

'Always the hero.' Roger teased, nudging Chris lightly. He walked away with a box of items in his arms.

'You're one of a kind, Chris.' Greg was still crouched at the base of the tree and Chris gave him his hand, helping him up. 'It's what you do for love.' Greg instinctively moved to free his hand once he was standing, but Chris held on. 'Some things are just worth fighting for,' Chris said quietly, his eyes steady on Greg's. Then he turned, chin lifting in the direction of the barn where the soft sound of Linda's piano drifted out into the afternoon. He gave a small nod, then finally let go of Greg's hand.

Pappi's bridal gown was made of lace and silk, flowing gracefully around her. The intricate beadwork and delicate lace embroidery made her look every bit the loveliest bride her mother had ever seen. She had been allowed to sit in Pappi's room throughout the two hours that it took Sue, Mary-Anne and Jessica to fix the dress, and her hair. She couldn't have been prouder of her daughter.

Linda sat at the grand piano soothing everyone's emotions with her skillful playing. Then the doors of the barn opened, and Pappi took a deep breath, her bridesmaids dressed in soft blush dresses walking slowly behind her. As she walked towards Chris, Linda played *'Jesus, Joy of Man's Desiring'* by Johann Sebastian Bach. Chris's groomsmen - Roger, Tony, Greg, Patrick, and one of his two older brothers stood proudly beside him, smartly dressed in their tailored suits.

Pastor Joe officiated the wedding. He was the vicar of the old village church, where Pappi's father had once been the vicar. He was now saying, *'Chris and Pappi, as you stand here today, remember the love that has led you to this moment, the love that couldn't be quenched through thick and thin.'*

And as the sun went down he pronounced them husband and wife.

Chapter 40

Past and Future Meet

Pappi peeped out of her window to see Michael emerging out of his car. His wife followed him to the house. She and Chris had been invited to Rosina's triplets' birthday dinner which was held in Timotheo and Njoki's home. They would also be attending meetings in different parts of Nairobi. Rosina's triplets were lounging on the veranda with soft drinks in hand, enjoying the early evening breeze. Though now eighteen years old, there was still something endearingly childlike about them, especially today, on their shared birthday.

Caleb, the only boy and the quietest of the three, leaned against the railing sipping ginger ale. He didn't say much, but when he did, his comments were laced with a dry wit that often caught people off guard. Clare was perched on the arm of a wicker chair, legs crossed, narrating a story to their grandmother about dormitory drama. Clarissa sat beside her, occasionally chiming in to correct or add to the tale.

'If I had a shilling for every time someone said 'triplets' today, I could skip uni and retire.' Caleb said to no one in particular, staring into the horizon.

There was a beat of silence, then a burst of laughter from the adults nearby. Clare paused mid-gesture and threw a popcorn kernel at him.

'Too profound for someone who's still got a term to go,' Clarissa said with mock severity.

Caleb gave a slight smirk, still watching the fading light. 'The system's just not ready for my kind of education.'

Pappi listened to the voices downstairs and on the veranda as she made her way down. When she reached the base of the stairs she straightened her back, and gave her hand to Chris, who approached the stairs when he saw her coming.

She was seeing Michael for the first time after twenty seven years. He stood to greet her, taking her hand in his and clasping it gently between both of his palms. 'How have you been all these years?' He asked. There was kindness in his eyes, which surprised Pappi. Kindness was not a virtue she remembered of his.

They sat down to dinner and Pappi found that she kept a smooth conversation going with Michael and his wife. They talked about work, about events that she had been hosting recently connected to the project that brought her to Kenya. Rosina and Bernie were engaged in conversation with Chris, who looked over at where she sat and blew her a kiss. Pappi smiled at him, grateful that he had come back, and this time for more than a month.

The following day they would be visiting the Ruai community, to see the work being done by Jane, a social worker they'd been introduced to. After meeting at Uhuru Park at nine in the morning, they loaded sacks of rice, potatoes, carrots and various fruits into a Nissan. Timotheo had given his driver for the day, who'd be driving them to Ruai and back to Ngong Hills. Jane was a lively woman in her sixties who had worked in community service for decades. She informed them during the drive that the condition of living in many parts of the Ruai community was not the worst in the country, but that there were many desperate elderly people and youth.

'Many of them are mentally unstable. Some are sick, as you will see. They have suffered great tribulations, and are unable to work. We are trying to offer them counselling services and to help them to start small scale businesses.'

Pappi was thoughtful for a moment. Then she asked, 'Besides your food support, how else do they survive?'

'They have children and grandchildren who work to support the family. They also grow food in small gardens or rely on neighbors and friends. They do whatever is needed to survive.'

As they drove past the river in Njiru, Pappi felt like she was in a far away part of the country. It was surprising that there were still expanses of land in Nairobi, untouched by squatters or unclaimed by factories. Then she noticed the small iron sheet shanties scattered nearby the road.

'People live there?' She asked quietly.

'Oh yes.' Jane said. 'These are land-grabbers. They set themselves anywhere and with time they begin to build brick houses, so that one day they can claim the land as their own.' And she pointed to one such brick house, built as if the family would be settling down any time. Pappi was appalled. *Settlers. Land-grabbers.* She turned to Chris, who stared out the window as lost in thought as she was.

As they drove through the villages, crowds of children and adults surrounded the vehicle, trying to get Jane's attention. She was known to them by name. Working for the government was esteemed in some areas and respected. However Jane did not only earn her respect from working with the government. She was also a pastor. In her work as a pastor she promoted high moral values and encouraged many villagers to return to their Sunday school teachings about the Christian faith. In a country that was heavily corrupted, the Church was the only institution that many people felt they could trust.

Now Jane ordered the car to be stopped and unwound the window so that she could speak to a group of women that were waving. She turned to Pappi and Chris to explain: 'These women are doing fundraising for a rehabilitation building project.' As she turned to speak to the women in Kikuyu, Pappi could see young boys jumping up and down trying to see what was in the back of the vehicle. She was eager to begin to unpack the food into bags for them.

Finally they stopped outside a roadside market where they would be able to reach more people. Jane had a team in Ruai, who were waiting at the market square. The team worked non-stop, packing and issuing foodstuffs and at the same time dealing with problematic individuals. Several drunken people came by, and Jane's team dealt with them. Chris and Pappi watched them in great admiration. Chris noticed that there was always someone - usually a woman, though sometimes a man - who wanted to see her privately to discuss a domestic issue.

'She could use help. I don't think they're paying her enough to deal with all the problems brought to her.'

Pappi agreed. 'Can we do something?'

'That depends, do you feel this is your place?'

'I am not sure.' Pappi said thoughtfully, 'but if the funding comes through, we'd have resources to help her hire someone to organise and lead her team. That way she could concentrate on what she feels is the most important thing.'

Chris agreed it was a thoughtful idea and he said so. Adding, 'But perhaps today we're here to learn?'

Pappi smiled at him. 'Today we're here to learn.' She agreed.

At around half past four in the late afternoon they drove to the yard of an old couple whose life situation Jane had described during their drive from the city earlier that day. The rest of the team had driven back to Ruai centre for refreshments. Jane handed Chris and Pappi bananas and coke, and bottles of water. The house was partly made of cardboard, and partly of mud. The part that was made of mud had big holes in it so that you could see a fire going, and someone bending over it.

Jane called out just as they slammed shut the car doors - it was the way of things here. A woman who looked to be anywhere between sixty and eighty stepped out, a wide, toothless grin lighting up her face. In one hand she held a wooden spatula; the other she stretched out warmly to greet the guests. Her eyes were strikingly bright, showing no signs of illness or hardship. Her husband sat in a corner of the two-room house. Up on the ceiling was storage for firewood. Below that was a low bed on which lay their pregnant daughter. Rumours had travelled fast during the afternoon that the social worker and her team had arrived. Jane usually came by to bring the special package of foodstuff for this home, and always a pot of steaming milky Kenyan tea awaited her arrival. Because of the heat Pappi found it difficult to enjoy her mug of tea. To be polite, Chris drank both his and hers.

The tea went on for well over half an hour, and Pappi was pre-occupied in her mind during this time. The conversation carried on much in Kikuyu, with Jane translating to Chris who was keenly interested to know how on earth the family managed under the circumstances they lived in. Pappi wondered if learning a vernacular language would be helpful to her in the future in Kenya. She knew her mother must have been from the Kikuyu tribe because the predominant language in Njoro was Kikuyu.

She couldn't help wondering how they might support the pregnant woman and her soon to be four children. All six of them lived in this small two-room house. Their main source of income was trading the produce from their small scale farming which was obviously not sufficient for the family's needs. Pappi knew that should they decide to take in the pregnant woman and her children into their project, they would need to develop a support plan for the elderly couple, who evidently depended on their daughter and grandchildren for survival. She made a mental note to discuss this with Chris once they got back to Ngong Hills.

The journey back was an exceptionally long one because of the traffic, but also because the day's events had been exhaustive.

Jane and Chris did much of the talking on the way back. They discussed ways that they could raise immediate funds through crowdfunding. When they parted at Uhuru Park Pappi promised to contact Jane in the coming weeks.

Chapter 41

The Road Ahead

It was Sunday morning in the last week of September. Pappi was sitting up in bed with her laptop, having finished replying to all the emails she had received in the last month following their visit with Jane to the villages of Ruai. Looking back on the last weeks Pappi realised that they had already made some progress. She smiled as she realised too that this was nothing like what she had in mind when she planned the trip. What Pappi had seen in Ruai had left questions in her mind and she had found that she could not move on yet before she returned to the Ruai villages.

She had compiled a brief report of her visit and sent this to friends and colleagues who supported her project. Chris had written personal emails to their close friends, informing them that the funding had come through, and that they had paid for a land they'd spotted in Maralal. Sue had insisted on sending financial help for the old couple that they had visited in Ruai. Tony and Jessica had suggested opening a charity account for the elderly who lived in poverty.

This developed an idea Pappi had been having since her visit. She had spoken to Jane regarding the rehabilitation centre that was being set up for young people. The centre would cater for the recreational activities as well as provide skills for developing small-scale businesses. The more Pappi thought about this the more she felt that the end results of the centre's vision may not be as fruitful as many people hoped. From what she had seen so far of small-scale traders in Nairobi there was not much room for development to meet the rising needs of families.

She spoke to Chris about this.

'Well, what do you propose?' He asked.

It was the day they were going back to Njoro, where they'd be for a week before proceeding to Maralal.

'I was thinking,' Pappi sighed, 'What if we'd try to get a licence for establishing educational institutions? We could establish one in Ruai and one in Maralal.'

Chris thought about it. He said, 'As easy as it seems to establish schools and what-have-you in Kenya, darling, we wouldn't know where to start, would we? Or would you? And, the thing that complicates it further is that we're not citizens.'

She came and planted herself on his lap. 'I know. But maybe Timotheo knows someone that could help Jane expand her *'Team Ruai'*. Wouldn't that be excellent darling!'

He wrapped his arms around her, 'Brilliant. But I am sure Jane can expand her team with no help at all.' He observed her with fascination. Then said more seriously, 'You should focus now on Maralal. We're already investing a lot there, and spreading ourselves too thin might compromise the quality and impact we aim for. I'd say we focus on consolidating our efforts in Maralal before further expansion. Quality over quantity, my love.' He kissed her, glad that they were retreating to a small rented cabin in Maralal, where perhaps she could take a break from planning things.

PART 4

The Work

2004

Chapter 42

Cafe *Fika*

The influx of funds for Cafe *Fika* in Nakuru had begun coming in March, setting a positive tone for the upcoming months. *Fika* was Sue's idea. In Swedish it meant coffee-break, and in Swahili it meant to arrive.

'*Fika* suggests a place of arrival', Pappi said in delight. 'I love it!'

'I told you it was genius!' Sue said proudly.

After Sue passionately shared the café's mission to help struggling young mothers in Nakuru with her network, support began pouring in.

Spending much of their time in Njoro and Nakuru, Chris and Pappi grew increasingly attached to the idea of working closely with low-income families in the region. The struggles these families faced were evident, and the number of children and youth who had dropped out of school due to financial hardship were staggering. It soon became clear that a multi-faceted approach was needed to meet the diverse needs of the surrounding communities.

Café Fika was set to open in May, with the goal of providing work opportunities for local young mothers. Pappi and Chris decided that establishing a branch in Njoro could offer vital support to low-income families located closer to home. Beyond employment, the café would serve as a community hub, hosting educational support programs to help youth gain the skills and knowledge needed for a brighter future.

Roger was overseeing the plans for the construction of an educational institution in Maralal. Since he fully became part of the project, licences came through within months. They were building a large Secondary Boarding School that would provide study places for youth from that area and from other northern locations in Kenya. It would be an investment for the future, offering hope to low-income families who had long struggled with limited access to education.

Chris had convinced Pappi that collaboration with colleges in Nakuru and Njoro was the best chance they had to have an impact in that region. They had secured a substantial number of supporters who were enthusiastic about supporting the construction of a technical school in Njoro.

'About Fika Cafe,' Chris had started. He sat across from Pappi at the kitchen table, a map of Rift Valley spread out on the table. 'I've been giving this a lot of thought, and I think instead of constructing a new building we should consider renovating an old one.'

'We've gone through this, Chris.'

Chris nodded, 'I know, but hear me out. It would reduce the demand for new construction materials, and minimise the environmental impact associated with new buildings. Additionally, repurposing an existing structure aligns with sustainable development goals - which we want to make sure comes out clear in everything we do. Besides,' He closed the map and put it aside, 'My leave from work ends in July, and realistically you won't be able to oversee any projects effectively in Njoro and Nakuru one-handed.'

Pappi knew he was right. Just then Greg called, his lively banter livening up the mood.

'Pappillote, love!' He yelled.

'Greg!' she chimed in, her voice filled with cheer. 'Are you in the neighbourhood then?'

'Yes, I am, love. In the neighbourhoods of Sydney.' He laughed, 'I'm visiting my boys.'

By the end of their conversation, Greg had generously donated £1500 to support the initiatives in Nakuru and Njoro. Not only that, but he also put Keith on the line, who also sent a donation.

A few weeks later Pappi received heartfelt emails from Greg's daughters, Dorothy and Candy, expressing their eagerness to help with Fika cafe's initiative in the Rift Valley. Pappi wasted no time in extending an invitation for them to visit, which would allow them the opportunity to see the place and meet some of the young people whose lives would be benefited from all the donations and the work of the cafe. The months ahead held the promise of progress as support continued to flow in, fueled by numerous speaking opportunities that Pappi had in different parts of the country.

Chapter 43

Rest, Re-fuel, Reconnect

The sun hung high in the Rift Valley sky as Tony, Jessica, and their eighteen year old son Albert, made the long journey from Jomo Kenyatta airport to Njoro. *Jessica isn't like Mary-Anne or Sue,* mused Pappi as she prepared the two guest rooms upstairs. The night before they arrived, Pappi had been on the phone with Mary-Anne, trying to figure out what it was about Jessica that was different.

'She's just more sure of herself than the rest of us.' Mary-Anne had offered.

'No, it's not that.' And then a bit annoyed, 'We're sure of ourselves, aren't we?' Pappi had retorted.

'Yes, but look, she's lived in South Africa all her life, Paps. She didn't have to re-root herself some place far away from home, you know?'

'Oh I'm sure she was uprooted and re-rooted right there in South Africa more than we know.'

'Nonsense.' Mary-Anne snapped. 'What is it with you anyway? Are you a bit jealous of Jessica?'

She didn't know what it was she felt, but soon after they arrived she did. One afternoon, with the scent of freshly brewed Kenyan coffee wafting through the air, Pappi found herself buried in plans for an upcoming event. Her desk was strewn with papers and colour-coded schedules. Jessica found her furrowing her brow, scrutinising every detail of what was before her. She leaned casually against the door frame, her coffee cup in hand. She observed Pappi's tense shoulders. Taking a sip of her coffee, she ventured in saying in a friendly voice. 'It looks like you've got the weight of the world on your shoulders. Let me help you.'

Caught off guard by the sudden intrusion to her thoughts, Pappi looked up and managed a weary smile. 'The usual chaos. You know how it goes.'

Jessica raised an eyebrow. 'Sometimes you have to let go a bit. You're good at what you do, but you don't have to bear it all on your own.'

Pappi sighed, setting down her pen. She leaned back in her chair. 'I know you mean well, but just now all I need is to get this done.'

'And I want to help you get it done.' Jessica had perched herself on the edge of Pappi's desk. She continued, 'Guess what kept my parents Home for Kids afloat?'

And there, she knew what it was that bothered her. *Mary-Anne will be happy to know there is a reason why Jessica's family were never uprooted*, Pappi thought. *They were doing all the right things*. To Jessica she said, 'You gave them sound advice?'

Jessica was astonished, 'I suppose I can be a bit overbearing at times. But if I were buried in so much work and someone offered to help me, I wouldn't get offended!'

'And I hear you, Jess. Sometimes I want your help. Just this,' she waved her hand over the desk, 'is something I have to clear first, on my own.'

Chris had returned to London, and in his absence, Jessica and Tony had come to help Pappi and Roger manage the load. Their son Albert spent much of his time cycling and assisting at *Café Fika*. Tony had travelled with Roger to Maralal for a field visit, leaving Jessica at the house with Pappi and Timotheo who was in town for two days to see a few old buildings they were considering buying in Njoro and Nakuru. Jessica now nodded. 'I'll leave you to do your work if you promise to holler when you need help.'

Pappi grinned, 'Wait. I'm sorry, I can be unbearable too. And,' She paused, pulling her thick hair back with her hands. 'While you're good at and quick to give advice, I'm not good at receiving it.'

With a mischievous glint in her eye, Jessica began, 'I knew there was nothing wrong with my advice!' They laughed. 'You must learn to receive advice though, Paps.' Pappi picked a crumpled-up paper and threw it at Jessica, who said as she went away, 'You need my help!'

When Pappi had sent those letters in 2002 to her friends around the world, telling them about her plan, and introducing them to tentative ideas she had for a development project in Kenya, Jessica had been one of the first people to contact her. 'I assure you,' she had written on behalf of herself and Tony, 'you'll have more people interested in supporting this work than you are aware of.'

Jessica had been right. From Australia, Pappi had received emails from Greg's network who had thought the work she was doing was noble and 'deserving absolute support.' Greg had assured her that himself and his house - which included Linda - were behind her one hundred percent. Her own colleagues from the law firm in London had contributed substantially, and a few had flown in to see the development of the work in Maralal.

Timotheo was about to drive back to Nairobi. They stood outside Café *Fika* in Nakuru which nestled modestly at the edge of a leafy lane, its wide windows gleaming. There were small outdoor tables shaded by green umbrellas. A wooden sign with hand-painted letters swung slightly in the breeze, reading '*Café Fika - Rest, Re-fuel, Reconnect*.' Many stopped for a quick meal or a moment of calm over a cup of tea or coffee. The landscaping was simple - flower beds edged the gravel parking area, and a small herb garden peeked from the back. Timotheo looked around, clearly impressed. He commented, 'Pappi, if you want to go into business, talk to me - I'd be delighted to work with you!'

Pappi laughed. 'It had nothing to do with me.' She said, 'I have good friends, who have good friends. All I have done is share my vision with them and they ran with it.'

Chapter 44

Empowering Dreams

She'd met many nice people in Nakuru and Njoro in the last weeks. Ndirangu and his wife Miriam reared chickens for sale to local restaurants and residents. Pappi had met Ndirangu at the market place and he had asked her if she was the new teacher at the local school.

'No, I am not.' Pappi had answered. Then, 'why do you ask?' out of curiosity. He laughed good-naturedly. 'You look like a teacher,' He had said.

'I do?'

'They said there's a lady from Europe at the high school across from the big church. She's teaching the students how to make candles - very good ones, I've seen them myself. Last week they were here in the marketplace, selling them. Good for the children to learn a skill they can use after school.'

Pappi had become interested and stood at his stall to chat.

'I have a boy in high school. He's proud of his new skills,' He laughed. 'Candles are still useful in many homes - especially the kind they are making.'

'Do you have other children?" Pappi had asked.

"Yes, I have three others" Two daughters and a younger son who'll be a doctor when he grows up.' He laughed.

'How nice! How about the others? Do they know what they want to be when they grow up?'

'One of my daughters wants to buy a lorry and transport goods from place to place.' He said in a dismal tone. Pappi understood he considered driving a lorry a less-ambitious dream.

'A girl, wanting to be a lorrydriver!' She said cheerfully.

'That's the problem. Who'll marry a girl like that.' He clicked his tongue, a look of distaste on his face.

'A determined girl like that,' Pappi started, 'Every man will want to marry.'

A few days after meeting Ndirangu, Pappi and Chris met Miriam, and who warmly welcomed them to Njoro. Miriam was a well spoken woman, often finishing off her husband's sentences. She became the main supplier of eggs to Cafe *Fika*.

With this and few other encounters with local residents in Njoro and Nakuru, Pappi felt ready to face the work of the project ahead of her. It was late October and she was travelling to Maralal, where Greg and Roger were, supervising the laying of the foundation for a Primary School and low-rise apartment buildings. With EU funding secured, they had been able to purchase an additional 30-hectare plot of land in Maralal, and the vision that Mary-Anne had at the very beginning was steadily turning into a reality. On the way Pappi spoke with both Mary-Anne and Sue. Mary-Anne was in higher moods than usual. She had a tendency to speak too fast when she was excited.

'Imagine all the things we could teach at the school! Secretarial and basic computer skills to the women and older girls. And oh, how about accounting? I've been training Patrick's staff for several years already - I'm well equipped to give some lessons!'

'Let's take one step at a time. Besides, have you both made up your minds when you would be coming?'

They'd be coming in December. Sue would be helping to set up a Cafe *Fika* outside the new High School site in Maralal, which was ideally located by the main road. She'd work with the local women of that area.

Chapter 45

Maralal

They slept in tents in the open plateau. The small hillside town of Maralal lay east of the Loroghi Plateau, and was the administrative headquarters of Samburu County. The once arid land was now a bustling construction site. The buildings were beginning to take shape, each layer of brick symbolising a step closer to their goal of providing affordable housing for many poor families. A large facility was being constructed in the heart of all the apartment-buildings that were springing up, which would serve as a kindergarten for the younger children.

'I still don't know how useful that will be,' Greg was saying. He had opposed the idea for a separate early education facility, citing that the women would feel deprived of their children as the custom was that they reared them at home until school age. They sat on picnic mats outside their tents.

'I'm sure the space would find another use,' Tony started.

'Early education is important. You'll see how quickly the women will get it.' Jessica said. 'It was just as difficult when schools were first introduced in Africa. Traditions didn't see any need for formal schooling. But look now - so many families are eager to get their kids into school, if only the schools are made affordable.'

They agreed, although somewhat uncomfortably. Roger stretched out on the grass, his head resting on his right hand. An amused smile played on his lips, and a blade of grass dangled casually from his mouth. Except for him, everyone was a non-citizen of Kenya and he knew they were aware of the colonial undertones in Jessica's statement.

'Change of that magnitude always meets resistance.' He said, 'But the villagers will appreciate the results, albeit decades later.'

With Timotheo's help, Roger had hired a skilled team of construction workers from a company in Nairobi, which was bringing the architectural blueprints to life. There was a deep sense of satisfaction as they walked through the construction sites. They had come a long way from their teenage years in Kenya, and a shared vision was all it took to get them all back in the same country.

Gathered around, they enjoyed a lavish meal prepared by their hired cook. They chatted with ease, laughter rippling every now and then. This time, Tony was narrating a story. He began by setting the scene - a grand party he and Jessica had attended in Johannesburg.

'So, there we were,' Tony was saying, his animated gestures emphasising each word, 'at this swanky soirée, hosted by a peculiar businessman of some sort, who had a thing for the bizarre. I'm talking exotic pets and a collection of hats from around the world.'

'Now, picture this,' he continued, 'we're mingling with the guests when suddenly, a parrot wearing a tiny tuxedo lands on my shoulder. I kid you not! It starts squawking, *Polly wants a cracker,* right into my ear. I nearly jumped out of my skin!'

Laughter erupted around the fire, everyone envisioning the absurd sight.

'But wait, it gets even better,' Tony continued. 'Our eccentric host decides it's time for a parade of his hats, and guess who he recruits as his 'models'?' And Jessica, unable to hold still shouts, 'Us!' and continues to tell the story, 'One by one, he plops these outrageous hats on our heads, each more extravagant than the last.' Tony imitated the host's flamboyant style and mimicked the hilarious hats, everyone roaring with laughter.

With the punchline delivered, Greg belted out the lyrics of the Beatles' timeless *Let It Be*. His voice filled the night air, and when he forgot the lyrics Patrick stepped in, and all the others joined in. The night continued with renewed vigour.

PART 5

Expansion

2006

Chapter 46

Pursuit of Health

Pappi was in Nairobi for some important meetings, as well as to receive donated items. Everything had been carried out to the waiting truck - computers, printers, scanners and countless books and stationary. The College in Njoro had been set up in an old school building that they purchased in February 2005. Many of the items were jointly donated by M.A.T & F and the university of Nairobi.

She would be having a meeting with the minister of health at the KICC. Their first meeting the previous year had not been very pleasant, and having left with a feeling that she had pried too closely, she was very surprised to receive a phone call, inviting her for another discussion. With him was going to be the well known Doctor Okoth of the Nairobi Hospital, who was mostly known for his research on HIV.

During their first meeting, Pappi's main initiative had concerned the welfare of less privileged people, especially the women and children's health. In particular she had wanted to highlight Maralal, where they were encountering all manner of health problems among the women and children. The meeting had resulted in a dead-end confrontation. The minister had insisted on an ongoing equal distribution of health care in all towns, which was far from equal, and which neglected all Pappi's arguments based on her own and Roger's findings.

Pappi's truck stopped at the KICC parking lot and she got off. She took a deep breath and brushed off curly hair that had strayed over her eyes. When they saw her, they stood up, smiling, and shook her hand.

'Pappi. It is good to see you again.'

'How do you do,' Pappi said.

'Now. A cup of tea, or coffee perhaps?' The minister laughed boomingly, saying something about how much coffee Westerners consumed, and how little of it was drunk by the Kenyans who grew it. Pappi was not sure if she was classified as a Western in this respect, but having been accustomed to Kenyan humour, she didn't give it much thought. A discussion was stirred up about the origin of coffee, the sending of it to England for processing and blending and the resending it back at high costs for consumption by the Kenyan elite, or the Westerner that lived in Kenya.

'But back in the day, eh, we drank *Kahawa* number 1. No problem.' The minister and Dr. Okoth laughed. Back in the day was before he rose to the status of politician, when access to coffee ended at Kahawa #1.

Pappi had been right in affirming that investigation of the health standards of the women and children in less privileged conditions had not been fully carried out, and that many of these people not only lacked access to medical care but also were not aware of existing help programs. There had in fact been a program running now almost a year and half in every town in Kenya, which the minister of health had vaguely been referring to when he claimed that the distribution of medical welfare was equal in all the large towns. Doctor Okoth had been involved in the development of this program and was now working towards making this possible also in smaller towns. There were difficulties of course.

'I dare say we have some money for this to be carried out in roughly about two towns at the moment. We have selected a number of these already, carefully taking into consideration the population of each town, the health status, etc etc. But how to implement this without causing disturbances by the many towns that consider theirs to be in greater need?' The minister was saying. Pappi was taking this in and thinking it over as he continued. 'Keep in mind that a dedicated team of doctors need to be found, who will be willing to work under harsh conditions, poor infrastructure, and low pay.' Everyone was silent. The minister of health moved forward, clasping his big hands in front of him.

'What you're actually saying is that there are no sufficient funds to fully carry out this work.' Pappi spoke into the engulfing silence that had momentarily filled the room. She continued in a louder voice, 'how much money are you talking about?' When she heard herself say that she almost stood up. She had no business nosing in this financial dilemma. All she wanted was for the ministry of health to wake up and do something about their dying women and children. 'I mean, do you have a plan on how to achieve this? Is there a way that the sum could be collected, say, by the end of the year?' Everyone was silent.

Finally the minister cleared his throat. 'I can frankly tell you Miss. Pappi, that we have not estimated how long it would take for all the towns to receive this same benefit as we are trying to implement in areas where there's more urgent need. The problem is that there are no expected returns, as you understand.'

That is actually not a problem, thought Pappi. There are never any expected returns in terms of money, as she was sure the minister meant. 'The expected return,' she said, 'Is the better well-being of this group of people.'

'Of course,' the minister agreed, leaning back in his chair, with a look that suggested he saw a possibility for a resolution.

'There has got to be another plan that brings in money, that keeps the projects running - buying medical equipment, transportation, paying the doctors' salaries. There's got to be a plan.' Pappi said, almost ruefully because it seemed a dead end. She had been there in some of these places where desperate mothers and fathers stood by their sick children and helplessly waited. Many of them had no hope. They'd watched too many of their loved ones die for lack of medical care. Many lived so far out of reach from civilization that transportation to the nearest health centres was by feet or in the arms of good Samaritans.

'This is why we need you Miss. Pappi.' The minister declared. 'How?'

'You have a big plan that we can tap into. If you can include this urgent medical care for women and children into your plans for Maralal and the larger Rift Valley areas, we can help you to get enough doctors.'

'What about resources?' She looked from one to the other.

'Our understanding was that you have been granted funding for this purpose by the European Union.' Doctor Okoth said. The minister laughed. Pappi laughed.

'Gentlemen. The funding we received covers the implementation of what we are already undertaking - the education work in Maralal. Part of that funding now covers the college in Njoro and also has funded the rehabilitation centre in Ruai.' She spread her arms helplessly. 'You need to have a bigger plan than tapping in!'

More tea was poured out, and fresh samosas were brought in. Somehow the men had relaxed more and now as they ate Pappi saw clear faces, hers included. She was consumed with the need for a breakthrough. The tea break was much needed. As they drank their steaming mugs of Ketepa Tea, they talked about feedback from those who worked on health projects in towns outside of Nairobi. There was improvement in most of these towns, and although there still was demand for increased salary, the nurses were content with their work. What was feared was whether or not the doctors would be able to continue for a prolonged duration of time especially in the wake of many invitations to private hospitals.

'Since my time is running out,' the minister said, looking quickly at his watch, 'I must leave you to continue this discussion, and for Dr. Okoth to update you on a certain plan.' He gulped down his tea and stood up, taking Pappi's hand in both of his and saying kindly, 'Miss. Salmon. We're delighted at your return home, and we support all your plans. Please,' he said, with his right hand on his heart, suggesting undivided dedication to what he was about to say, 'Let us work together.' With that he left, leaving Pappi to wonder if there was something she had missed during their conversation.

It turned out they had a magnificent plan for raising funds for a continual health work in many small towns and villages in the country. The next two hours included lunch, which went mostly untouched, perhaps since they had just filled themselves with samosas, but also because of the intensity of the discussion at hand.

'Dr. Okoth, with all due respect I cannot accept this responsibility. You're asking me to put aside everything I am doing at the moment and concentrate on something that I had not thought through in such depths - it's impossible. I'm sorry.' Pappi shook her head vigorously as she sat back in exhaustion.

More land was in the process of being purchased in Maralal with plans for cultivating it, because the irrigation system had proved a great success in the past year. The inhabitants of the area lived on livestock herding, but many were interested in learning modern ways of cultivating land and using the irrigation systems. Pappi couldn't see herself putting this work aside and embarking on something new.

'What the ministry of health is asking you is simply to oversee a work that we believe you could do better than most. Concrete plans have been made already and what we did not tell you is that there are funds set aside for 10-15 doctors' salaries. Key people have been found to oversee various tasks – constructing health centres, drilling wells, infrastructure. What we need is someone to bring these together and oversee the overall work.'

She could not make a decision of that dimension in an instant, and the doctor understood this.

'When I came to this country my goal was simpler than what you are asking of me. I do not feel qualified for this task, and although I support it a hundred percent, I cannot give you an answer immediately.' Then in hesitation she said, 'I cannot promise that my answer will be what you want to hear either, because my husband will have a say in it too.' The doctor leaned forward with an outstretched hand. He smiled as he shook her hand, 'It's enough that you give this a good thought. We shall wait to hear from you.'

The journey to Njoro was unusually long. Pappi kept drifting back and forth between the projects, thinking of the order of their importance. There's not one of them she deemed as less important. In the educational centre in Nakuru over 300 had gone through various training sessions in the past year. These included young mothers and youth, who were learning everything from basic computer skills to cooking and baking. Eleven youth had so far been assisted in finding work outside of the community. This inspired many more into enrolling.

Chapter 47

Danish Pastries

Pappi neared the market place where she would get off to visit Cafe *Fika* while the truck driver proceeded to unload at the College. She could see a late evening queue through the glass door, and Wambui busily moving about. Several young women worked in shifts at the Njoro Café. Two of them were single mothers who also attended classes at the College. Because they worked part-time, Wambui was largely left to run the place. Pappi crossed over to the back room where Sue was winding up her evening class. She smiled and waved, mouthing, 'I'll wait in the cafe.' Sue scowled at her and brushed it off, saying loudly, 'We're done for the day anyway,' and then to the women, 'Check on your Danish pastries ladies, if they are done wait for them to cool before packing up a few and leaving the rest for Wambui to freeze. Thank you for the day!'

They went to the small back office that contained a small desk and two chairs that were from the Farmhouse. All over the walls were recipes printed or handwritten. Pappi stood, trying to make sense of Sue's handwriting, listing all kinds of pastries. Since the day they had set up the sign outside Sue had felt right at home. That was two years ago. Greg's daughters had been a great help in setting up the place and designing posters for advertising it. Pappi thought how fast time had passed. Just the past year Greg and Linda had stayed five months, up until after Christmas, teaching at the college.

'Danish pastries?' She eyed Sue.

'Yes, we're 'travelling' through northern Europe now, and this week we're in Denmark.' Sue smiled, thinking there's never been a more satisfying career than the one she was doing.

'Outstanding,' Pappi said thoughtfully.

'Think of it. These girls - and the women who come to these classes - have never googled any country abroad. They're learning things about other cultures in an interesting and delicious way.' She laughed.

Pappi sat heavily in the chair. 'Have I told you you're a genius?' then before Sue could reply, 'I'm in a fix and you have to help me.' She sighed.

'You're always in a fix.' She was making hot chocolate and getting an apple pie from the small fridge.

'Here.' She handed Pappi a piece of pie and some whipped cream she had made. She then poured out hot chocolate in two mugs, adding thick cream into each cup.

'Your problem Pappi, is that you don't know when to say no.' She stated. Pappi was sipping her hot chocolate, wondering if they shouldn't be watching their weight at their age. She glared at Sue for a moment before defending herself.

'Yes I do!'

'You don't.' She stood to shut the door that was agape. They could hear the clinging and clanging of utensils in the kitchen and the excited noises of the last customers.

'If you wanted, you could have let this drop way back in June last year. You didn't need to go along with it. You're not a doctor, Paps, there's other people that could do this.'

Pappi drank her hot chocolate. It was impossible to separate the health needs from the other needs that she had to deal with in the projects.

'What do you propose I do?'

'Honestly at this point just go with what Chris tells you.' She shrugged again. 'I'm not saying health is not as big a need, I'm just saying you can't do everything. Needs will keep showing up, and you've got to know your limits.'

'Jessica!' Pappi exclaimed. 'She's a doctor, she might be interested in taking this offer!'

Sue stared at her. Then, 'Yes!' she exclaimed back.

And then a moment later, 'Only they have a son still living at home and I don't see him eagerly following them into the wilderness.'

'Albert is a man already, he'll be happy to be left behind.'

'I'll give Jess a call tomorrow, see what she thinks.' Pappi said. 'I haven't committed myself to anything. But I can't ignore the fact that the health issue is something that must go hand in hand with the development of these projects.' She shut her eyes and leaned back. 'I keep seeing a throng of people on their way to semi-arid areas.' She whispered.

'What?'

Pappi sat up. 'Four years ago Mary-Anne came up with an idea that Chris and I thought was overambitious and impractical. She had suggested converting the semi-arid areas into liveable environments - building residential houses complete with infrastructure and all main services, such as a health centre. Providing for the homeless a place to call home.'

'Well, we modified that impractical vision into something more feasible.'

'Think Sue.' Pappi's voice was edged in urgency. 'One of the main problems has been finding doctors who would be willing to go into remote regions to help the people. If the financial bit is taken care of, the main concern will be finding the doctors.'

'I'm listening.'

'How many young people leave Kenya every year for further studies abroad? How many are studying medicine abroad, getting jobs and settling there, never to return?'

'Countless.'

'Exactly! If we could find a way to make them come back home.'

Sue was shaking her head. 'You've got a knack for brain-benders, Paps, more than anyone I know.'

Pappi was trying to figure out where they'd begin. All she knew was that this sounded right and the more she thought about it that evening and the next and the following week, the righter it felt.

Chapter 48

West Pokot

They sat out on the terrace of *Cafe Paradise* in the little town of West Pokot. Greg kept his arm firmly around Linda's shoulders, casually rearranging her hair like a privacy screen every time a German tourist looked too long at her bare shoulders. It was late November 2006, and the group had set off from Njoro two weeks earlier, visiting several sights along the way - including a five-day safari - before ending up in West Pokot. Chris and Roger had something to show them. They had been eyeing a piece of land in the area, which they were considering purchasing.

'What for?' Greg asked, looking over the desert land that was bare and uninviting.

'I can imagine that with good irrigation the land could sprout crops,' Tony began, 'but don't we already have enough work in Njoro, Nakuru, and Maralal?'

'It's not a project,' Roger beamed.

'Well, what?'

Roger and Chris looked over at Patrick. 'Tell them, Pat.'

Patrick wiped his brow and took in the thick, hot air before speaking. 'Well, ladies and gentlemen, since we're here quite often, we thought it best to consider having a holiday place of our own.'

There was a stunned silence. Jessica blinked, as if trying to determine whether she'd heard right. Greg let out a soft whistle, while Linda chuckled and said, 'You mean, like a timeshare?'

Tony looked from Patrick to Roger to Chris, squinting against the sun. 'You're serious.'

'How?' Greg stood, spreading his hands in a wide circle to gesture at the bareness of the land all around.

'By making an oasis in the desert, transforming the inhospitable into magnificent holiday homes. And,' He pointed his finger, immersed in his inner vision of what they had in mind, 'making these thirsty places hospitable.'

'And the resources?' Tony began.

'Uh! The money,' Patrick, his entrepreneurial spirit kicking in, couldn't help but see potential in the barren terrain.

'In reality,' he was saying, 'my company is willing to invest in this Holiday Homes idea, but it all hinges on one crucial factor - income generation. If we can ensure that the venture is a sustainable business, then we're on.'

The vast expanse of the desert stretched on and on beneath the unforgiving sun. They arrived at their campsite near Mount Mtelo. The tented camp was established in 2004 by a group of local entrepreneurs, to promote sustainable-tourism and cultural preservation. They were occupying five of the six large canvas tents, which were raised on wooden platforms. Bucket showers and pit latrines were located at the edge of the campsite. As they chatted in the shade of a sycamore fig that first evening, the conversation turned toward possibility. The notion of developing Holiday Homes in a desert began to take shape - not merely as a retreat for tourists, but as a gateway to something more enduring. The desert held an undeniable appeal for travellers seeking unique experiences.

'Or researchers,' Pappi found herself speaking her thoughts aloud. She had known about the idea for some time but had waited for Chris and Roger to share it themselves. Now, hearing it voiced around the campfire, she felt genuinely delighted by the idea.

'You're right,' Roger said, 'The potential here goes beyond tourism. With the right marketing, we could attract researchers, conservationists, and travelers looking for authentic, off-the-grid experiences. Greg's firm could help us reach that kind of international audience.' He winked at Greg who was still processing the idea.

Over the next four days they explored every aspect of the Holiday Homes concept, from design and construction to marketing and operations. They considered the challenges of sustaining such a venture in the harsh desert environment and the need for eco-friendly practices to ensure minimal impact on the delicate ecosystem.

Tony mapped out potential features and layouts for the Holiday Homes. They envisioned structures that blended with the desert environment while providing modern amenities for guests. Pappi wondered how they could involve local communities and ensure the venture benefited the region. She imagined cultural exchange programs where guests could truly experience the desert's rich heritage.

It was their final night at the camp, and dinner had been laid out under a clear sky, now full of bright stars. Lanterns flickered, illuminating the long wooden table where the group gathered. A few solar-powered lamps lined the path to the wash area, barely noticeable in the vast darkness. After hours of lively discussion and ambitious planning, a natural quiet had settled over the table. Pappi sipped her tea, her thoughts drifting.

It had been weeks since she had been offered to oversee the health project by the Ministry of Health. While considering the offer, Pappi had come to the conclusion that she wasn't the right person to lead a project she didn't feel fully qualified for. She had given them a counter offer. Doctor Okoth and the Minister of Health had listened intently as she shared her proposal for a policy-driven approach to incentivize Kenyan doctors abroad to return to Kenya, alongside scholarship schemes targeting students from low-income backgrounds.

'What you're saying is good. But wouldn't that risk making it more difficult for Kenyan students to pursue medical studies abroad?' Doctor Okoth asked.

'Not at all - that's not what this is about,' Pappi explained. 'It's about creating strong incentives to come back - real opportunities at home that make the choice easier.'

The doctor leaned back, nodding thoughtfully. Then he looked at her and said, 'Miss Pappi, if you and your team can help us, I have no doubt that our Kenyan doctors abroad will come running back home.' He had his finger pointing at her. 'Didn't you come running home?'

'I did,' she smiled, 'though as my husband says, I came to a country that doesn't recognise me as its own.'

'Ah my friend,' The Minister waved his hands. 'You're not the only one. Our policies are complicated, and as much as I'd like to tell you that we'll issue you and your friends dual citizenship, I cannot do that. Not yet.'

Pappi was not expecting him to do miracles where their citizenship was concerned. It could be another decade before Kenya accepted dual citizenship.

'The West offers more than a higher salary, Minister. You know that. It's the life-style. The association with something that attracts people. If Kenya is seen as a forward-moving country, where solutions are created and progress is real, the entire diaspora will be drawn home.' She now leaned back and assumed a more relaxed posture. 'I was a member of the student union, back in my university days at the University College Nairobi. The vision we had in those days was of a powerful country that was globally competitive. Kenya had just received her independence and everyone's dream was of rising up to the standards of the Western countries, and beyond. We believed it was within our reach.'

'Then you left.' The Minister said, rather flatly.

'But I came back.' Pappi responded defensively, 'In London I've lived amidst immigrants who left their countries in search of something greater than what they could find at home. They made home in a country that wasn't theirs and gave their best to it, neglecting without a thought the condition of their own countries.'

She leaned forward, 'Minister. I could find a team that could work with me in this for results you haven't thought possible. What I am asking you now is to find a way to bring the Government on board. Together we will create a joint team which will begin a campaign throughout the Embassies of Kenya around the world, attracting Kenya's talent back home.'

The Minister's mouth fell open. 'How do we do that?'

Pappi smiled. 'I have a team that can achieve anything they set their minds to.'

PART 6

Together

2007

Chapter 49

Dynamics of the Team

Two days before Tony left they sat in the coffee room of the Study Room, which is what the college was now called. It was the last week before Christmas and many of the women who normally studied half day were now staying for the long full-day classes. Schools were out for vacation and for them it meant that they could leave their little ones at home with their older siblings who were home for vacation. The group was having coffee and tea and a variety of cakes and bread that came in every morning from Cafe *Fika*. Earlier that day they had spent an hour at the construction site in Nakuru where the foundation was being laid for a new Study Room and a larger Cafe *Fika*. The current facilities were getting smaller as the groups increased each term.

'So,' Greg was summarising. 'Are we in agreement?' They had been discussing a proposal to the BBC, exploring the possibility of co-producing a short documentary on Kenya's urgent need for medical care in remote regions. Elizabeth would be helping to submit the proposal. The film would follow Kenyan medical students studying abroad, juxtaposing their journeys with the work of their peers at home. It would highlight major health development projects in Kenya - goals set, progress made, and the Ministry of Health's vision to reach the country's most inaccessible communities. Greg's son Brian, a media professional, had joined the team overseeing the project's development.

'Yes!' Tony banged his fist on the table.

Mary-Anne said, 'For the first time I am doing something meaningful with my life.'

Linda put a hand on her shoulder, 'All the work you've done here in the last months, May, you're amazing.'

Pappi was speechless. The way everyone had taken this as their own responsibility was beyond her. In the Netherlands, Sue - accompanied by three students from the University of Maralal - was visiting institutions of higher education, speaking about collaboration. She advocated for the university, which now offered a nursing degree, and highlighted the work being done there.

They were in Jyväskylä University of Applied Sciences, in Central Finland. Anticipation filled the air as students streamed into the auditorium. The crisp winter had left Sue's team's hands numb, and now as the auditorium filled, they each clasped their coffee cups to warm themselves. They were passionate advocates for healthcare initiatives, and were eager to share their experiences.

The Head of the university expressed a keen interest in collaborating with the university. She saw the potential for students from both countries engaging in exchange programs, sharing knowledge and experiences that would benefit all involved.

Sue called Pappi that night. 'Tell me, did I promise too much?' After having described the discussion she had with the university, of the possibilities of joint research projects, internships, and capacity-building initiatives. 'No.' Pappi assured her. 'I think Roger will agree that you did just the right thing. Think, if we have just one successful partnership, our reach will have a great impact and very likely another round of funding.'

Chris was in Belfast with his team of educators from Maralal and Nakuru. They were visiting towns within Northern Ireland and the Republic of Ireland. This sort of thing was not new to Chris, who had worked closely with the Crown Institute of Deaf People in the end of the 1990s to bring awareness to the lack of integration between the deaf and hearing youth communities. This last week he had said to Pappi, 'It doesn't matter that this health project is besides what you had in mind to do when you first went to Kenya. Look at the work you've already achieved.'

'We,' Pappi had said with emphasis. '*We* have achieved. All of us.'

'You're right. We.' Chris continued, 'I had no idea that banking was not the way for me, until I followed you to Kenya.' He laughed. Pappi was silent, then she said, 'I wouldn't have done any of these without you. And you - sacrificing decades of banking.'

'It wasn't a sacrifice at all.' Chris assured her. 'It was time for me to do something that gave me reason to get up in the morning. And I'm not the only one who feels this way,' He added with emotion.

'No?'

'Darling, look at all our lives. Which one of us is not enthusiastic about our work?'

He was right, Pappi smiled thoughtfully.

Each member of the team had taken on a role that reflected their expertise and their shared commitment to building something lasting. Pappi remained committed to shaping long-term strategy, and making sure that everyone - from the government to local communities - was working together. Chris and Patrick oversaw finance and institutional development across Maralal and the Rift Valley, focusing on sustainable financing through grants, investment, and key partnerships.

Roger headed the University of Maralal, guiding its academic direction and forging its identity as a center for rural innovation. Tony, still based in South Africa for the time being, headed a small interdisciplinary research team linked to the university, focusing on rural healthcare systems and sustainable community development. Jessica, a medical doctor, planned to continue her work in Maralal where she and Tony would be moving to when the time was right. She would also collaborate on research and strengthening training within the university.

Greg took charge of communications - crafting the public image of their work and leading engagement efforts locally and abroad. His wife, Linda, focused on cultural programming, developing initiatives that promoted cultural exchange. Mary-Anne had stepped in as the new head of the college in Njoro, bringing with her a strong sense of academic leadership. And Sue was actively strengthening ties with universities and organisations around the globe, advocating for meaningful international collaboration. They were building a model that was rooted in local strength and global cooperation, of what sustainable, community-led transformation could look like.

Chapter 50

The Woman With A Dream

It was Sunday afternoon, and the village was vacated. The Salmons seemed to be the only ones left. They were not going anywhere for vacation. Her parents were away at church. Often Pappi had friends over straight after youth church. But today was different because no one was around. As she wondered what to do with her time the doorbell rang. Before she could get there it opened. Chris stood there in his beige shorts, looking flustered as though he was there by mistake. Pappi was flustered too. Of all the people he was the one person she had least expected to see. But hoped, and even prayed to see. Chris was just about to say something important to her when the alarm jostled Pappi out of her dream.

She slummed the alarm off and lay there with her hands pressed to her eyes. 'Silly dream.' She laughed out loud as she slipped out of bed and into her robe. Chris slept soundly beside her. It was half past five in the morning and she had a long drive ahead of her to Nairobi for what she hoped was the final negotiations for a new land in West Pokot. As the warm water ran through her hair Pappi wandered off to her dream. The house had something to do with it, she thought. There were memories packed up in every room and virtually every corner of the property. Although it looked different now after the renovations and all the work done in the barn and in the garden, it was still the same homestead she grew up in that carried all the memories of her youth in it.

Chris had woken up to see her off. She quickly kissed him, took a sip of his coffee and dashed out. He'd be going to Maralal himself, for a conference with the management team and their stakeholders from England. The stakeholders included Patrick's company, and they would also be discussing the plans for the Holiday Homes investment.

Three and a half hours later she arrived in Nairobi. She got out of her car, in a rather sceptical mood, to meet the people who, for the last ten months, had refused them purchase of the land in West Pokot.

She had been to countless meetings of this kind since her return to Kenya that at this point she was dried up of clever mental dialogues. It had been her custom to walk the remaining distance engaged in an intense dialogue that ended up in her favour. Now she walked slowly, deliberately, knowing she was two minutes early. When she reached the room, she learned that several attendees were still on their way and was asked to wait. Fifteen minutes passed. A tall gentleman entered and took the seat directly opposite her. She sat upright, meeting his gaze with composed restraint as he leaned forward, as if to speak.

'Miss Salmon? I thought it was you.' The man smiled, concluding it was her. 'By the way,' he stretched his hand and gave what Pappi thought was the most generous smile she had seen in a long time. She shook his hand.

'My name is Zachary Patricks.' His smile broadened.

'You're here about the land?' She asked in a straightforward tone.

'I am.' He gave a nervous laugh. 'And from the sound of it, so are you.'

Before they could continue, four men entered the room, carrying bulging folders. They took seats at the far end, flipping through documents. Pappi recognized one of them from an earlier meeting with the local lands committee.

The discussion that followed was surprisingly brief - but it was not without tension. Mr. Zachary Patricks, as she now knew him, presented first. He came well-prepared and spoke of development, of sustainable housing, and hinted at a potential eco-tourism angle. His polished proposal had weight, backed by urban investors and a clear financial roadmap. The committee members listened with respectful attention. He'd done his homework.

Then it was Pappi's turn.

She laid out her folder of correspondence with village elders, notes from field visits, and a community consent letter signed just weeks prior. She presented their plan for a satellite health centre, staffed by graduates from Maralal University nursing program. She spoke plainly about need and the meeting of that need.

One committee member asked whether her team had the funding for such an undertaking. 'We have enough to begin,' she replied. 'And we have partnerships with people who will come when they see that we've taken the first step.'

There was silence after that. Not the kind of silence that follows uncertainty, but one that acknowledged what had just been said.

An hour later, the decision came. The land would go to her and her team.

During their research of Pokot, they had found that they were not the only ones interested in the area. Unknown affluent people had not hesitated in making this a *Stepford neighbourhood*, building oversized mansions that were hardly lived in, in the midst of scattered mad and thatched huts. Most of the new landowners were absentee investors from Nairobi, drawn by the promise of real estate security, not community development. Most of them were city dwellers who had saved enough money to secure their children's future in real estate. They were also businessmen, like Zachary Patricks, out to make money. The difference was that *they* were also motivated to help bring development to this remote part of the country, and they had proof of what they could do. That was what got them the land.

'Darling, the land is ours!' Pappi was exclaiming on the phone to Chris. In the next ten minutes she recounted the entire meeting, and now instructed Chris to inform everyone of this great news. She was on her way to have lunch with Njoki in Westlands before her drive back to Njoro. There was so much traffic however that what would normally take twenty minutes took an hour. As she neared Westlands shopping centre Pappi saw the cause of this early-afternoon traffic. There seemed to have been an accident and a crowd of people surrounded what Pappi made out to be a blue Volkswagen. She drove to the side of the road and got out.

A small girl of about four years lay on the road, a red scarf over her. Pappi immediately rushed through the crowd and knelt by the little child.

'Is she alive?'

Several answers from the crowd that Pappi did not make out before the ambulance came and attendants shouldered their way through the noisy crowd.

'She's alive,' she said to them. The child was hauled carefully on the stretcher and carried to the waiting ambulance.

'Are you the mother?' someone asked her.

'No. Wait -' She rushed back to the crowd and loudly asked, 'Who is the mother?'

The little girl lay in a hospital bed in Kenyatta Hospital.

Many years ago Pappi had delivered Elizabeth in this hospital. She sat outside the ward, waiting for the doctor to come out with news about the little girl. There hadn't been any relatives among the crowd, and someone had said that the girl had been spotted walking alone a few minutes before the accident happened. Several people had said that she had been begging for money in the shopping centre. Some believed that she was a street child, left to beg by her mother or older siblings. Two hours had passed since the girl was taken in at the hospital, and there was still no news from the parents of the girl, and none from the doctors, on her progress.

Pappi walked to the cafeteria and bought a cup of coffee. Her shoulders ached and a slight headache was on the way. She reached into her handbag and fumbled around looking for aspirins. She took a tablet and drowned it with a mouthful of coffee.

'Miss?'

Pappi looked up eagerly. 'Yes?'

The doctor pulled a chair next to her, stretched his hand in greeting. 'Sorry that you've had to wait so long. We've had a shortage of doctors the last month, but not to worry. I understand the little girl is not a relative?'

'No. I came along since there were no relatives among the crowd. How is she?'

'She is stable, for the moment. We don't quite know if she has any head injuries since she is still in a coma. She is going to have to remain in intensive care for several days, and we will keep a close eye on her condition. Meanwhile we are trying to locate any relatives or guardians.'

'If I could be of any help, do not hesitate to call me.' Pappi reached for her bag and took out a card. 'May I see her?'

There were no cuts on her face or hands. She lay there motionless. Pappi took one little hand, praying silently that she would live. As she left the hospital she experienced a deep sorrow. She drove slowly out of the hospital grounds.

She had met many suffering children in the last few years that came from severe poverty. Pappi parked her car and made her way to La Piazzetta. A waitress greeted her with a warm smile, and led her to where Njoki was seated.

'Pappi, what an incident!' Njoki exclaimed, rising from her chair to embrace her friend. Pappi had called her to inform her of her delay and the reason for it.

'A distressing experience,' she said empathetically. 'I hope the child recovers quickly.'

Their conversation shifted to Pappi's work in the Rift Valley and Maralal. Njoki said with admiration, 'Most of us wake up to the same job we detest, and without a question we do it year after year. But you,' Just then Pappi received a phone call.

'She's out of coma!'

The two women stood to leave, excited beyond words. Pappi was thinking how relieved she felt that the little girl did not die. As they walked away, the waitress that had ushered her in watched them leave before they'd ordered their meals. She recognised the English-Kenyan woman who'd been featured recently in an article in Daily Nation. *The woman with a dream.*

PART 7

Bloom in the Desert

2009

Chapter 51

Desert Oasis

Christmas was a special season in Njoro town. A large Christmas tree had been put up, a donation from the Study Room College. Njoro and Nakuru towns had seen a great number of changes in their communities. The government had opened funds for the reconstruction of main roads and re-carpeting of some smaller roads. Large amounts of money had also been spent on renovation of several buildings such as two large schools, some government offices and a hospital. The Hospital had been extended and the number of doctors increased. This was not news any more in the country, which had welcomed almost three hundred doctors and nurses from overseas in under a year, and almost each one of these had been placed in a hospital or Health Centre. Dozens were still coming. Over half of these were above forty years old and most had said during interviews that they had '*thought of returning home many times, but it just never seemed possible.*' Citations of bad working conditions in Kenya and zero chances of work development were mentioned by many. Some had said that once they had left Kenya, they had not looked back, and never planned on returning.

Early Friday morning found Pappi sitting out at the porch with a cup of tea between her palms. It was two days to Christmas, and they'd be celebrating in West Pokot with their friends. She had been up since 5am, and could now hear corks crowing in the neighbouring farms. Dogs were barking and occasionally a cat ran wildly through the hedge along their fence.

She was thinking of the little girl that had survived from the accident, way over a year before. Njoki and Timotheo had taken her in because no one had come to claim her, until a week ago. A year into the adoption process, the biological mother of the little girl had resurfaced, her DNA confirming her parentage, and she had reclaimed her daughter. But not without a fight. Njoki and Timotheo, unwilling to relinquish the child who had come to occupy a space carved by past grief mobilised every available resource to retain custody. Timotheo's influence extended into corridors of power, and thus he pursued every legal avenue to prevent the child's removal from their home. However, the legal framework governing child welfare in Kenya as established in the Children's Act of 2001, affords primacy to the rights of the bio-logical parent, provided that parent is not demonstrably unfit. The High Court upheld this principle, concluding that despite the delay in the mother's reappearance, no legal grounds existed to permanently sever her parental rights. It was a devastating loss for Njoki, whose determined efforts to fill the void left by her son's passing had found, in the little girl, a fragile restoration. One now irretrievably taken from her.

Pappi went back inside. Chris was up, she could hear him walking up and down in their room. They'd be leaving for West Pokot in an hour. Everyone was already at the Desert Oasis, which was the name they had all finally settled on calling the holiday homes.

'It feels so good to call it something other than the Holiday Homes.' Pappi said, once they had started their 230 km drive to West Pokot.

'Hmm.' Chris smiled.

'Or Resting Homes.' Pappi shivered. She couldn't remember which one of the guys had suggested the name, which was instantly rejected by everyone. They were all nowhere near retirement. Or death.

After a taxing week at the colleges in Njoro and Nakuru, they were both looking forward to reuniting with their friends. The afternoon sun beat with a radiant intensity as they arrived in West Pokot. They were stopped a few times by familiar faces of people they had met during the past year. Roadside sellers hurried to exchange greetings, and from a distance, one of the village councillors called out, motioning Chris to come near to where the elders held their meeting under a towering acacia tree. They stopped the car and got out. Pappi knew their customs by now, that women were not allowed in such gatherings, so she walked over to one of the shops.

'Miss Pappi!' cried Sarah, the second of three wives of Longolomoi, who owned the largest herd in their village. She was there alone, which was unusual.

'Sarah, nice to see you! Are you well?' Pappi leaned over the small window of the shop. The shop provided essential items that residents in the region could not produce. 'I am well! And you know Miss Pappi.' Sarah leaned over, her head popping out the small window. 'It is now the *Sapana* season. And my sisters are busy with the preparations. Today our sons are important men!'

Pappi congratulated Sarah. *Sapana* was the rite of passage that allowed young men the right to marry and to own property, hence elevating their status in the society. Every shopkeeper that Pappi stopped to speak to had a celebration to go to, or one that was being prepared in their home. There was also a Christmas presence in the town displayed by the decorations outside shops and even a tall plastic Christmas tree near a square. Pappi marvelled at the community's unity and the hardworking women who were early at the market everyday.

'All is good with the men?' She smiled at Chris as they continued driving.

'There's a slight situation,' he said with a worried look.

Since they set up a Study Room in the region that taught skills such as technical skills and practical nursing, many of Pokot young men now had aspirations that were not the norm. The elders did not know how to deal with this situation. They had anticipated that this could be a problem, especially the clash of ideas and misunderstandings with the elders, who governed the way of life in the villages. To narrow the barrier, they had invited the elders as guests of honour during the opening of the college the past year. But it seemed that they had not fully understood where the new skills would be applied or where those new skills would be likely to take their youngsters. Many of the young men had expressed interest to move to larger cities for work after graduating.

'They do not have to leave the region,' Chris said. There were still no real opportunities for employment for 90% of the young people that would be graduating in two years.

'You're right,' Pappi said as they neared Desert Oasis. 'We could convince the County government to work with us in creating jobs for these young people.'

'We've tried that.' Chris shook his head. The Desert Oasis stood perched on the horizon, a retreat overlooking the majestic mountains. Among these peaks, the Kakwa Ard Mountain stood out, its imposing presence casting shadows over the surroundings. The sunlit untarmacked road led them through the changing landscapes, from scrubby vegetation to lush green irrigated fields. Desert Oasis had been providing irrigation systems to several farms in the region, and this had done much to create good relationships with the local people.

The main building stood out with its white walls and large glass windows, a piece of modernity against the setting of semi-arid nature's grandeur. The sun's warm rays played with the glass, creating dazzling reflections. In the distance, they spotted Tony and Albert engaged in a spirited game of tennis on one of the well-maintained courts. Laughter and father-son banter floated on the breeze as they rallied back and forth. Above them, on a roof terrace overlooking the tennis court, Sue stood waving madly. Her contagious energy made Chris and Pappi feel instantly at home.

The holiday homes were strewn across the expanse, each a secluded haven promising quiet tranquility. Encircling the cottages, lush gardens unfurled in a riot of colour, their blossoms exhaling the sweet, heady scent of exotic flora. The pools shimmered enticingly under the afternoon sun, while from a nearby sports ground drifted the lively echoes of spirited games and friendly rivalries.

Desert Oasis had become a hub for locals as much as it was for tourists. The sports facilities were open for use by the locals, and the pools offered respite to both locals and foreigners under the searing sun. These were also a wellspring of employment opportunities for many.

As they walked toward the main building, taking in the breathtaking surroundings, Pappi felt a profound sense of contentment.

'So we try a different approach.'

'Food insecurity concerns could be a new bridge maker,' Chris said instantaneously, as though reading her thoughts. She looked up at him, her hand instinctively finding his. He continued, 'We just need to think on how we can convince the local government and the elders to be part of securing a sustainable relief program.' He finished, drawing her hand to his lips and pressing a kiss upon it as they entered the building.

About the Author

Naomy Hyvönen was born in 1977 in Nakuru, in Kenya's Ri Valley,  and spent her early childhood in this richly diverse region before moving with her family to Nairobi at the age of six. Her formative years unfolded within the social and political climate shaped by the leadership of President Daniel Toroitich arap Moi, Kenya's second president, whose long tenure would leave an indelible mark on the nation's governance and societal structures. Growing up amid the complexities, contradictions, and evolving political philosophy of President Moi's Kenya profoundly influenced her understanding of power, reform, and the dynamics of political transformation. It is within this milieu that her lifelong curiosity about governance, socio-political change, and African studies was born.

Naomy completed her primary and secondary education in Nairobi, she went to Arya Girls high school where her passion for literature and societal questions began to flourish. In 1997 she moved to Finland to pursue higher education, where she studied Communication and English Philology, and expanded her academic journey to include Political Science and much later, Multidisciplinary Language Expertise. She also studied in Holland and worked in Belfast, Northern Ireland in the end of the 90s.

Naomy is a mother to two sons, and resides in Espoo, Finland. Her writing is deeply informed by her multicultural experiences, the intersection of cultures, and her enduring engagement with questions of political evolution, identity, and societal progress. The Eve Years of Reformation is both a personal exploration and a thoughtful contribution to historical reflection, inspired by the lived realities of Kenya's past and its ongoing journey towards transformation.